MW01071465

Halls of Horror
A Ten Story Collection

Dale T. Phillips

ISBN: 1470162318
ISBN-13: 978-1470162313

Kamikaze Hipsters was first published in
Dark Valentine, Winter 2010
Rummy was first published in House of Horror, Nov 2009
The Pit was first published in Ethereal Gazette, Dec 2007
Carnival of Pain was first published in Dark Valentine, Oct 2010
Locust Time was first published in Fungi, May 2011
Moose Tracks was first published in
An Electric Tragedy, July 2011
Body English was first published in
Gluttonlumps Chilling Tales, Oct 2008
Bless Me, Father, by Matthew Phoenix, was first published in
Necrotic Tissue, Apr 2009

Other works by Dale T. Phillips

Zack Taylor Mystery Novels
A Memory of Grief
A Fall From Grace

Story Collections
Fables and Fantasies (Fantasy)
Crooked Paths (Mystery/Crime)
Halls of Horror (Horror)
Strange Tales (Weird, Paranormal)

Non-fiction Career Help
How to Improve Your Interviewing Skills

For more information about the author and his works, go to:
http://www.daletphillips.com

DEDICATION

CONTENTS

FOREWORD

What are you afraid of? Are all your fears external? Things That Go Bump in the Night? Are you afraid of war, monsters, cancer, death from an infinite number of sources? Some other person or happenstance that tears into you or your loved ones, something from outside of you that smashes your world apart? The End of the World, maybe. That's pretty scary.

Or maybe you're afraid of what lies within yourself: the Mr. Hyde that lurks inside us, with ravenous appetites for destruction. A fury that can be unleashed by a traffic altercation, a divorce, a taunting remark in a bar.

We live in a world where many experience real horror with dismaying frequency. Some of us are lucky enough to escape that, and find our entertainment in stories where someone else is menaced. The horror tale has a long and noble tradition, handed down from our cavemen ancestors, who told stories around the campfire. Maybe back then it was wolves that were the menace, or that weird sound that came from over the hill. We know that horror can come from a known thing that is terrible, but far worse is something not known.

Fear is all around us. We fear what we cannot control, and so our world is a place of constant fear that something or someone might get us. The crazy mugger with a knife, the car accident, the doctor telling you about the spot he found on your X-ray. Maybe we don't have to fear otherworldly terrors, and so we focus on what we know we should be afraid of. We like the feeling of watching a character run for their life, as long as we don't have to do it ourselves. Here are some tales to let you feel that terror, that frisson, while remaining safe.

I had a great teacher when I was learning to write—Stephen King, the Master of the modern horror genre. He pulled the genre from the gutter, and gave it legs to shamble forth and disturb us all. He has many imitators, but few can write as well or as memorably. I certainly bow to his skill, and offer my own tales, along with some help from friends. This collection has different kinds of horror, and will hopefully leave you with some scary images to linger affectionately in your psyche.

The title for Kamikaze Hipsters came while I was waiting in a doctor's office, and in a morbid state of mind. I started writing without having any idea where the story was going. The direction came along in due time, and provided a tale of suffering for art. Katherine Tomlinson, who was editor at Dark Valentine, loved the title and the tale, and featured it with fabulous artwork.

Rummy is about the terror we have in modern society of not being successful, of losing our grip on the middle class, and being relegated to the horror of those who have failed. Astute readers will note the characters names are echoed in the annals of the labor movement in this country, a history that too many do not know about. There is meaning in that resonance, for without the sacrifice and protest of many faceless, nameless thousands who put themselves on the line in harm's way, we would not have the comfortable lives we enjoy. And yet we live in times where the loss of a job can well mean the loss of our livelihood, our health, and possibly our families. High stakes indeed.

The Pit poses a situation of dire peril, where a man is trapped underground. It gets worse, though, for there is something else down there with him. The dead may be the lucky ones…

Carnival of Pain is a flat-out homage to Ray Bradbury, especially his masterwork Something Wicked This Way Comes. If you haven't read it, you should. The carnival represents the darkness from outside that comes to town as a menace, and has been done many times.

Locust Time is a story with a central image that sticks in the minds of people long after they've read it. I had a bit of help on the ending from Pierre Comtois, editor of Fungi, who suggested the way to keep the first-person voice to tell of the final horror.

The Last Battle is a tale of the ultimate horror, war. For more than ten thousand years we've been killing each other, with no end in sight. Maybe we should think about alternatives to mass murder while there's still some of us left. This tale features a French soldier in Vietnam, but not the first French army to suffer defeat, and not the last invaders of Vietnam to suffer defeat. You'd think that some could learn from terrible mistakes, but humans are slow to catch on. After the Great War, it was thought to be the War to End All Wars. And yet the same idiots who had lost almost an entire generation of young men went back to slaughtering each other barely twenty years later, and created another World War. Plus ca change…

Moose Tracks comes from the Allagash of Maine (the state where I grew up), and where I heard tales of these creatures and how dangerous they are, despite their placid appearance. After this story was first published, I heard even more stories about moose encounters. Makes you wonder…

Body English is a story I originally wrote when I was taking writing classes from Stephen King. He liked the tale, which was a bit gorier then. I've since scaled back the nasty, but hopefully leaving enough in there for your entertainment.

The Silver Web is a Cthullu-mythos tale, the brainchild of my friend Tom Chenelle. His passion for the tale was such that I had to write it up, and I think it adds to the classic canon of the world of the Lovecraft lovers.

And for the last tale, Bless Me, Father, we have the first published story by talented writer Matthew Phoenix. This story was so well-liked by Necrotic Tissue, that they raised the pay scale for it to that of a professional. That is the highest compliment in the short story world of small markets. It's a fun little tale, with some sly humor to go along with the scary bits.

I hope you enjoy these stories. Certainly hard-nosed editors with little money to spend liked them enough to pay for them and feature them in their magazines for their readers. You've got quite a screening for the work you're reading.

KAMIKAZE HIPSTERS

Fueled by a combination of nicotine, caffeine, Benzedrine, and various additional pharmaceutical boosters, I got myself ready. With a testosterone bravado born of desperation I made my way downtown. Dressed in careful, pre-determined casualness, I passed along the sharp, wet streets, another pinball in the crowd, bouncing between the bumpers, inhaling the human odors in their marinating glory.

My destination, the Watkins Gallery, was in a rundown neighborhood far along in the process of becoming gentrified. The money moved in, and the tenants were swept out. Messieurs Watkins were showing my current crop of pain, along with the works of three other sacrificial victims, our guts on display for the gimlet-eyed plebiscite.

For me, I was done when the creating part was over, the rest meant nothing. But I had to work the crowd to earn enough sustenance to keep the wolf from the door. Somehow the public liked our artistic process. We ran our lives, dreams, and suffering through barrels of broken glass and nails, caught the shredded morsels that oozed out, and hammered the bits into pretty morsels for mass consumption.

5

Only one of my fellow showees was genuine enough for me. The other two were faux-artists, or Fartists, but the deluded hoi-polloi still fawned over their work. My own work was nearing white-hot status, everything I poured into my canvasses coming to fruition. Who would have thought Pollock-like spatterings of blood and bits would attract the flockers? The gallery catalog hinted at some of the darker elements in my work, enough to assure my cutting-edginess. I would catch the sidelong looks, fear blending with the admiration, those timid sheep wondering if the rumors were true. I tried to look feral and demented when I smiled back.

I wearily endured the crowd. There were the middle-aged matrons with little knowledge and no taste, but plenty of money and the desire to rub elbows with real talent. The common crop of art students, yearning to add depth to their callow lives. The slim, bearded men, with black turtlenecks and gray ponytails, speaking of Foucault and the neo-whatever of the moment.

I ground my teeth into a smile as they complimented me on the crap I had issued, including the series I called "Failure." There were nine of them, abysmal all, but these sheep lapped it up as Ambrosia.

Then She appeared before me, with ninja stealth and suddenness, at once in my face. Blazing hazel eyes, short-cropped black hair, elfin face, trim, shorter than I, eminently courtable. Before I could run out the hook, she jumped from the water and smacked me with her tail.

"So the only two important things are Love and Death, and you get that, but looking at your work, I can't tell which you enjoy more."

And just like that, my cynical armor was so much useless tinfoil. She got it, she nailed my essence, more than the critics, the would-be explainers, more than anyone. She grasped the beating bloody heart of what I did, and held it up. Thanatos and Eros, the Siamese twins of my raison d'etre.

Desire swirled in the vortex of nature's wiring. Ah, nymph, in thy orisons be all my sins foretold. Come with me for the passion and the pain, my lovely. I am the bastard child of Casanova and Ted Bundy, and I will hide my grosser nature for a time. Dance with me in the cold moonlight on the cliff's edge. Let us share ancient poetry as we bleed each other by the candle's flame. We will burn and sear our crackling flesh until our heat consumes us and we crumble to ash.

But my glib cleverness is gone, the easy pickup banter that magnets the nubile hangers-on to my chambers. I am suddenly ashamed of the plastic cup of cheap Cabernet I am holding, and set it down. I rub my nose and point to the closest of my atrocities.

"What do you think of that one?" say I, solipsist bastard that I am. She smiles, a petite Giaconda, and glances dismissively at the ghastly thing at which I gesture.

"Did you urinate on that one while doing it, or afterward?"

She sees through me like a plastic wine cup, the little minx. As a matter of fact, I had, both during and after. Not the tourist-trade pieces for her, the ones that pay the rent and keep me in cigarettes.

"Where's a piece like 'Beckett'?" she says.

Oh, my, she does know me. That was a favorite, sold six months ago, detailing a blood-covered King Henry of England holding the naked corpse of his friend and victim, Good Olde Tommy Beckett, Archbishop of Canterbury.

"The Watkins does not encourage my more esoteric pieces." I smile. I want more of the bad wine, but also more of the dark frown that creases her visage.

"So you're slumming," she said. "Not like you. I was hoping for another 'Massacre'."

My God, if she had seen that piece without screaming for the police, she was definitely a genuine art lover. I had almost gone to jail over that one. Had I seen her before? Other shows? That talk I gave at the Crendell school?

Anything I could say would sound hollow and cheap, so I adopt a Zen-like silence, letting her come to me, the Mystery Man.

"Aren't you going to ask me to model?"

"Model?" I said. "I don't think so. My work leaves… scars."

"Yes," she says, her eyes never leaving my face. Her pale skin glows. She pulls back a sleeve to show me a long, white jagged worm on her arm. I run a finger along its length, aroused.

"I did that to prove a point, once." Her grin is wolf-like.

Damn, I am lost in her depth.

On the walk back, she takes the cigarette from my mouth, puts it in hers, and deeply inhales before returning it to me. I thrill to the Bacallian sensuality of the gesture, but detect no falseness, no ploy. She needs none, she is a force, pulsing with life. I am excited with the possibilities.

Her skin is flawless, but for the one scar, unmarked by tattoos, the betraying marks of instant street cred for the desperate wannabes, as if cool can be purchased with needle-and-ink. The dance is brief, our hunger abbreviating the preliminaries. We know what we are about, and we set to it. We are soon as one, smooth pale frames joined in an exquisite mix of pleasure and pain, nails and teeth rending numerous wounds, her knowing eyes drinking in my ecstasy and suffering. We shriek and sweat and bleed for an eternity.

Hours later, spent and pensive, the epiphany strikes like lightning. I realize what she is to me, and lean over to whisper into a blood-flecked, translucent ear.

"My masterpiece."

She shivers with pleasure, instantly knowing, instantly committing. "How will you do it?"

"I don't know yet."

"It's alright," she strokes my hair. "We have time."

And we do. My rooms are well-larded, our isolation complete. Cut off from the world, we do not leave for two days, and we are bothered by nothing but our passion.

Knowing what she knows and what is to come, she laughs, she sleeps, she eats without hurry or longing, she seems without regret or concern. She knows I will take her farther than any other, that all my previous work was merely practice for this. She is the original kamikaze hipster, flying into glory in a bomb-laden plane, a nuclear remembrance that will burst upon the world with our fame. I realize I cannot survive this apotheosis, that my career simultaneously reaches both its peak and its finale. I am delirious with happiness. This is truly, finally Art, my life's work, which I can finally realize.

I think on it more, and see beyond. There must be, will be two in the plane, a perfect melding.

We spend hours creating a carefully worded letter, then realize our folly and tear it up, giggling and giddy. The work is our message. Words would only sully it.

The time comes. We bathe, eat our meal, read each other poems by Mishima. In silk kimonos and bare feet, we pad out to the studio, with its impressive array of implements, and a giant canvas of porcupined Saint Sebastian overlooking our efforts. I have prepared more tools than I have ever used on any three works. They gleam in the studio lights. Each cutting edge or piercing tip is a brush, and we are the paint.

We place the folded kimonos to the side, beyond the range of spattering, and stand upon the sprawling canvas. Her eyes are bright as I pick up the first brush: a clean, well-oiled blade.

I embark upon my magnum opus.

Dale T. Phillips

RUMMY

Mike Morton paced back and forth by the restaurant door, shuffling through his sheaf of papers, awaiting his fate. He looked around like a prairie dog scenting the air for signs of approaching danger. "Big Bill" Hayward, president of the company, would soon arrive, and whether Mike would be working after the meeting was subject to Hayward's whim. Years of careful, hard work building a career and climbing the corporate ladder now depended on this presentation.

Mike was terrified at having his future in the hands of such an overbearing jerk. But in this corner of the corporate world, Hayward was the lead dog, the others ran behind. They ran on and on, in the hope that someday they would move to the front, and their view would change to the wide open plain of leadership.

Mike wanted that lead position as bad as the rest, but his stubborn streak of decency ran against the common ideal of a ruthless corporate magnate. Though he hated the petty, backstabbing viciousness considered a necessity at upper levels, he was more afraid of failure. His obsessive worry that he might end up discarded and forgotten like his father made him work almost 80 hours a week, including most weekends.

Unable to stop fidgeting, Mike went into the restaurant. He stopped to take several deep breaths, and looked around the place. Mike was startled to see that one of the busboys was a white-haired old man. He looked absurdly out of place in a busboy's white shirt, baggy black pants, and a black bow tie that drooped on either side. He was thin and stoop-shouldered, shuffling slowly around the tables. He picked up dishes with an exaggerated precision that failed to hide the tremor, likely caused by long-term alcohol abuse.

Mike was instantly reminded of his ruined father after the failure and the drinking. The elder Morton had shown the same signs of defeat. Mike drove himself, to avoid ending up the same way, and he glared at this old man with something approaching hatred. The man looked up, as if sensing Mike's gaze, and looked him full in the face. His eyes were bloodshot and pale, looking like watery poached eggs. Mike could not meet that gaze. He looked away, his revulsion giving way to pity.

Hayward came in, with three men in tow. Mike noted Winn, Renfield, and Sutter, and mentally dubbed them Young, Taut, and Ruthless. He decided that would make a good name for a law firm.

Hayward called out to the maitre d'. "Marco! Table for five!"

Annoyed diners turned to stare at them. The roomful of executives did not appreciate having a power lunch disrupted. Mike flushed in embarrassment.

Hayward and company were led to a large table in the back. Hayward frowned, and Mike knew he wouldn't like not being in front, where he could see and be seen by the other power players.

Hayward glared at the maitre d'. "This the best you got?"

"Sorry, Mr. Hayward," crooned the man. "You know how the lunch crowd is. If you'd called ahead, I could have saved one for you out front. If you want to wait, I can try to move you up..."

"I don't wait," snapped Hayward. "Tony will hear about this, that's for sure. All right, so be it. Everyone sit."

They took their places around the table. Mike arranged his papers in front of him, but before he could begin, the waitress arrived.

"Hi guys," she chirped. "I'm Tina and I'll be your waitress today. Can I get you something to drink?"

"Seven and Seven," Hayward said.

"Heineken."

"Same."

"Club soda with a twist."

"Iced tea," said Mike.

"Okay, I'll be right back," she smiled and walked away.

"Check out the caboose on her, eh?" Hayward chuckled to the others. Mike groaned inwardly.

"Hey, old buddy," asked Winn. "What's with the club soda? You on the wagon?"

"I'm in training. Got the bike race this weekend," replied Renfield.

Mike suddenly realized he had lost points. Power players didn't order iced tea, they ordered serious stuff, unless they had a status reason not to. The ritual helped establish the hierarchy, and now it was too late for Mike to correct the error. He would have to make up for lost ground.

Hayward spoke. "Morton here says we should keep him on, because he has a project that will be good for us. Isn't that right, Mikey?"

"That's right," replied Morton, feeling like a trained seal. Mike began his pitch, pausing when the waitress returned. He continued after they had ordered their meals, and saw that he soon had Winn and Sutter nodding agreement. Hayward said nothing, showed nothing, but let him finish.

"Not bad, not bad," Hayward said. "Of course, if we go through with it, that means we have to cut funding for someone else."

"I'm not convinced this is the right thing, Bill," Renfield said, looking down, as if afraid to speak his mind so boldly.

Mike found himself fervently hoping that the roof would fall in on Renfield.

"See there?" Hayward smiled cruelly. "Always looking out for his own. Renfield, this kid's coming up fast. You're not careful, he'll take you out."

Further business was put off by the arrival of the meal. Mike was jubilant at his apparent triumph. He hardly tasted his food. He wanted a drink.

The shabby old busboy shuffled up to the table to clear away the dirty dishes. As he reached for Hayward's plate, Hayward shied away in disgust. His clenched jaw made the cords stand out on his neck. The old man shambled away.

"Did you see that old rummy?" Hayward exploded. "I can't believe this!"

"Rummy? What's that?" Winn said.

"An alky. Alcoholic. Like a guy who drinks rum all the time." Sutter answered. "What's the matter, Bill?"

"Matter?" choked Hayward. "He's the matter! Didn't you see him shaking? We're lucky he didn't puke or spill something on us."

"Geez, Bill, he's just some old geezer trying to make a living," said Renfield.

"Well he doesn't have to make it here," snapped Hayward. "And let me tell you something." Hayward jabbed his finger at Renfield. "That old man stinks of failure. Sour, stale defeat. I don't like failures, and I won't have them around. I don't want that rummy at my table. In fact..." Hayward looked around, caught the eye of the maitre d', and beckoned him.

"What can I do for you Mr. Hayward?"

"Is Tony in?"

"Yes. Is there a problem?"

"Yes, there is a problem. Go get Tony for me."

Marco hesitated a moment before going. He cast a glance back over his shoulder, and Mike saw him question their waitress. She looked at them and shrugged.

Conversation at the table stood uncomfortably still until the arrival of Tony, an older, silver-haired man who spoke in dulcet tones. "Mr. Hayward. Always a pleasure. What can I do for you?"

"What are you doing to me, Tony?"

"I don't understand, sir."

"I ask for a table, we get stuck in the back, like something you're ashamed of. Then we get a bimbo waitress. But the worst of all is you have some broken-down old rummy busboy come slobber over us. What's the matter? You don't want my business anymore?"

"The busboy? What did he do, Mr. Hayward?"

"Do? It's the fact that he's here at all. You used to have good help."

Mike saw the shabby old man watching the exchange, staring with those watery, bloodshot blue eyes. His expression did not change. The man's fate was in the hands of Hayward, just as Mike's had been. Mike felt ashamed.

"I hired him this weekend," explained Tony. "He's just some guy down on his luck. Figured I'd give him a break."

"That's real decent of you, but what about your customers? Think we want to see that old rummy hanging around?"

"Sorry, Mr. Hayward. I'll see he doesn't work the lunch shift anymore."

"Tony, Tony," groaned Hayward, shaking his head. "If I come in here for Happy Hour and see this guy, suddenly I'm not so happy. If I come to dinner, and see this guy, I could lose my appetite. Tell me, am I a good customer?"

"The best."

"Right," smirked Hayward. "I'm worth a lot of money to you. The table, well, you're busy and all, the waitress, hey, we can overlook that, but this... this is like seeing a cockroach crawl across my plate. He's dirty. All I'm asking is, get rid of the cockroach. You understand what I'm saying?"

"I understand, Mr. Hayward. Sorry you feel this way."

"Well, you got a nice place here. I just hate to see things that make your customers uncomfortable. He doesn't really belong here now, does he? It would be better for everybody."

"I'll talk to him."

"Great, Tony, great. Hey, we'll see you tomorrow, right?"

"Sure thing." Tony left the table and walked over to the old man.

Burning with shame, Mike couldn't bear to watch. He stared down at the tablecloth. Hayward was jovial as they paid the bill. Mike excused himself when they left, claiming a telephone call.

When the others were gone, Mike found the owner. "Excuse me, Tony. It's about that guy. The one Hayward was talking to you about."

Tony's face hardened into something ugly. "What about it?" He said harshly.

"You don't have to let him go, do you? He didn't do anything. Hayward went off for no reason."

"What am I supposed to do?" Tony said. "Mr. Hayward drops a lot of money in here. He stops coming, I lose a lot. I tried to do a good thing, but it just didn't work out, that's all."

"So it comes down to money."

"Yeah, it comes down to money," Tony said, angry. "I got two kids in college, and two more going soon. I got bills to pay. What about you? You're with him. While he's telling me who to fire and how to run my business, you just sit there. What's the matter, afraid he'll fire you, too? I'd say that comes down to money, wouldn't you?" Tony walked away.

Mike flushed an embarrassed pink. He cursed himself for a coward and left. The old man was nowhere in sight.

Later that day, as he sat on the john in the restroom, Mike heard Renfield and Winn talking.

"Can you believe that Hayward?" said Renfield.

"Yeah, he's something. Getting that guy fired. He sure plays hardball," Winn sounded admiring, as if it were a great coup. "What made him do it?"

"What I heard," Renfield said, "is that Hayward's father was a drinker. Lost his business because of it. Lots of family troubles, too. Never got back on his feet. Hayward drinks, but can't stand anyone who reminds him of his old man."

"Pretty twisted," said Winn.

Mike started thinking as he washed his hands. Today had been the last straw. He wanted success, but could not exist in an environment like this. No matter how hard he tried, he could not fit himself into the mold like Renfield or Winn. If he stayed, he would get callous and then get ground up like all the rest. He headed to Hayward's office, realizing the craziness of what he was about to do.

"Come in." Hayward said when Mike knocked. Hayward was alone in the office, which looked out over the city, and sported awards, trophies, and executive paraphernalia along the walls. "Ah, Morton. What's on your mind?"

"It's about that man, the one you call rummy."

"Don't worry about him," said Hayward with a smirk. "You won't be seeing him anymore."

"That's the problem," said Mike. "What you did wasn't right."

"What did you say?" Hayward's eyes narrowed.

"He's just a harmless old man," Mike said. "There was no need to go after him the way you did. You were wrong to do that."

"Why you little pissant," Hayward rose from his chair, his face choked with rage. He poured out a stream of invective, as Mike watched him coolly.

"Well, if you're going to get emotional, I guess there's no use in talking to you about it," Mike said, turning to go.

"You can't talk to me like that!" Hayward screamed. Flecks of spittle sprayed from his mouth. "Do you know who I am?" He roared.

"King of the Jerks?" Mike said, and quickly left.

17

Ten minutes later, Renfield came in with a smile on his face like he'd just won the lottery. He told Mike that according to Hayward, Mike's services were no longer needed at the company. He handed Mike a box, and told him to clean out his desk.

The reality didn't hit until Mike was on the elevator going down to the lobby. His legs almost buckled as he walked into the outside world.

Standing on the sidewalk, blinking against the sun, Mike noticed the old rummy watching him from across the street. A taxi pulled up and Mike got in, watching the old man through the back window of the cab.

Back in his apartment, Mike set down the box and looked around. Tomorrow he would start looking for another job, but tonight he was going to get ripping drunk.

Morning came as a nasty hangover, a white, blinding pain that blotted out the rest of the world. Mike slowly rose from the floor where he had passed out. With a throbbing head, puffy eyes that didn't want to open, and his stomach churning in protest, he made it to the bathroom, where he promptly threw up. For several minutes he lay slumped by the bowl. Groping through the shower curtain, he found the faucet handle and turned on the water. The sound encouraged him to move into its path, and he groaned as the hot spray hit him. Opening his mouth, he let water run in, washing away the awful taste. He drank some greedily, and let the rest cleanse his face and run down his body. After a few minutes, he turned the faucet handle, and braced for the shock. Cold water hit him like a slap, and Mike gasped as it brought him to full consciousness.

With his mind now working through the pain, Mike got out and toweled dry. He took out a bottle of aspirin, shook four into his hand, and swallowed them with water from the sink. He went to the kitchen and put on a pot of coffee.

A short while later, with breakfast and the aspirin working, Mike felt less awful. He wondered what to do on his first day of unemployment. The rootlessness frightened him, for going to work each day had given him purpose. In losing his job, he had lost his identity. He wandered around the apartment, as if seeing it for the first time.

An hour later, as Mike was still trying to decide whether or not to get dressed, someone knocked at the door. He opened it to see two men in suits. The one in front was noticeably balding. The other, who hung back, was tall and thin. Each of them displayed a badge.

"Mr. Morton?"

"Yes?"

"I'm Detective Hill and this is Officer Vanzetti. Could we come in and talk to you for a few minutes?"

"Uh, sure." Mike stepped back to let them in. "What's this all about?"

"Mr. Morton, could you tell us where you were last night?"

"Last night? I was at Wobblies, the bar over on 23rd. Why?"

"What time did you leave?"

Mike tried to think back, but it was a blur after about ten o'clock. He flushed in embarrassment and shrugged. "Sorry, officer, but I really don't remember. I got pretty drunk."

"Problem?"

"You might say that. I got fired yesterday."

The policemen looked at each other, a quick, confirming glance.

"Is there anyone who can vouch for the fact you were there and when you left? Were you with anybody?"

"Not that I remember. I guess you could ask the other people in the bar. I must have taken a cab, you could find out from them." Mike looked at the men. "Why are you asking me these questions?"

"Do you know a William Hayward?"

"He's the company president."

"Not anymore. William Hayward was stabbed to death last night." They let that news sink in for a moment, before pressing on. "How do you feel about Hayward?"

"He fired me yesterday. But murdered..." Mike sat down. "My God."

"So you had a grudge."

"Well, not enough to kill him. Am I a suspect or something? Do I need a lawyer?"

"If you think you need a lawyer, go ahead and call one."

"I don't really know. This is all pretty strange."

"Mr. Morton, it's our job to find out who killed him. You had a motive. Is there someone else you know of who might dislike him?"

"Most of the people he came in contact with. He got someone else fired yesterday, at Tony's Trattoria. They'll tell you."

"Okay, we'll check it out. Anyone else?"

"I didn't know him personally. Only what I saw at work."

The policemen continued to question Mike for awhile before leaving.

It had been an inauspicious start to the first day of his forced vacation. Mike felt like a TV character. He tried to get his bearings, but his mind kept going back to the news of Hayward's death.

He knew he needed to get back into the swing, start calling around, but he didn't much feel like it. It was a Friday anyway. He would take the weekend off, and start fresh first thing Monday.

Since he wasn't going anywhere, Mike decided not to bother dressing or shaving. He read the newspaper slowly, and discovered when he was finished there was still a lot of day left. Without the focus of work, the defining point of his life since leaving business school, he had no idea what to do with himself. He made lunch and sat on the couch, watching television. And so the day passed.

When Mike finally noticed it getting dark, he sat for a long time before getting up to pull the shades and turn on a light. He was dazed, and didn't feel like cooking dinner. He ordered a pizza, and opened a beer. His system could take it now, and it tasted good. He finished the first beer, and opened another. By the time he was on the last beer of the six-pack, Mike had a good buzz on. He didn't have to think about work or death.

Saturday dawned bright and clear, and Mike was appalled that he'd done nothing the previous day. There was so much that needed doing. He showered, shaved, and dressed, determined to get things done. Action was the key. He shopped for the week's groceries, did some laundry, and ran errands, giddy with excitement and energy. Maybe he would call someone for a date, since he'd been too busy for one in the last two years.

Back at home, Mike turned on the TV news. He heard the name Renfield and turned the television up. The newscaster was explaining the terrible accident at the Tri-City bike race. Renfield had apparently missed one of the turns and careened off the road, landing on rocks fifty feet below. The newscaster said he had died before the ambulance arrived.

Mike went back to the kitchen, stunned. The world curled in at the edges. He took another beer out of the refrigerator. It turned warm in his hands before he finished it, but he didn't notice.

The story came back on during the eleven o'clock news, and Mike forced himself to watch it again, absorbing the details. It was the same story, the newscaster explaining in grave tones how it had happened. The camera panned to show the crowd, and Mike felt the shock of recognition when he saw the old man from the restaurant. The same wispy white hair, the stooped shoulders, the watery, out-of-focus eyes. Mike jumped up to confirm what his eyes had told him, but the camera had moved on.

It was too frightening to think about. He wanted oblivion. He finished all the beer, and then opened a bottle of whiskey.

Later, in his alcohol-sodden sleep, Mike dreamt. He saw the rummy shuffling up to Hayward in the parking garage. Hayward saw him and began to shout, reddening with rage. He took a step toward the old man, and suddenly stopped, giving a convulsive shudder. As he stumbled back, Mike saw the handle of a knife protruding from Hayward's stomach. The rummy reached for the handle and yanked the knife out, pulling down as he did. Hayward looked utterly astonished as he tried to stop the flow of blood with his hands. His mouth worked, but no sound came out. He fell back against his luxury car and collapsed to the concrete, arm reaching out in supplication. The old man then smiled. It was the most terrifying face Mike had ever seen. The rummy shuffled away as Big Bill Hayward spilled out his life on the oil-stained floor of the parking garage.

The rummy was standing in some bushes by the side of a road. Men on bicycles raced by. The old man remained hidden from view, though only a few feet away. Suddenly, he stepped into the road and thrust out his arms. A man on a bicycle was completely surprised, and the push sent him in a straight line off the road, instead of following the curve. He couldn't stop himself from shooting off the embankment. Mike saw Renfield's astonished face before the man cartwheeled through the air onto the deadly rocks below.

The rummy melted back into the bushes, again wearing that terrible smile. Mike shook himself out of the dream, waking up cold sober and gasping in fear. Had this been what had actually happened, or was it the result of his drunken imagination?

If it was true, then Mike needed to call the police. He turned on the light and reached for the receiver, then hesitated. What would he tell them? That he had seen the killer in a dream? Calling the police would make him more of a suspect. He thought about when Renfield had died. Did he have an alibi for that time? If he did, then he was in the clear, but otherwise he'd better not make the call.

Mike got up, turned more lights on, and began a frenzied search for all his receipts from the day. He turned out his pants pockets, went through the papers on the counter, and even checked the garbage. A grocery tape and a credit card receipt each had the time on it, and there was a laundry slip without a time. The paper trail was only partial, and there was a gap of more than two hours. Frustrated, Mike held his head in his hands. He couldn't do the right thing for fear of getting himself in more trouble. He would wait until the next day and see what he could do.

When he got up on Sunday, Mike was shocked to see that it was past noon. He still had not reached a decision, so he went for a drive to sort things out.

As he drove, Mike wondered how things had gone so wrong. It all stemmed from that damn rummy. Because of him, Mike had lost his job and was under suspicion. He was now a failure, a man tainted with the stigma of being fired. New employers would also suspect him. He was angry at Hayward, angry at the other executives who had so cavalierly tossed him onto the trash heap. He had fallen off the corporate ladder, and didn't see how he could get back on.

One thing he could do in his present situation was to clear his name. He would go to the police and tell them everything. If they caught the rummy, he would be cleared.

Mike went home and called the number Detective Hill had given him. Hill asked him if he would like to come to the police station to make a statement.

Mike was nervous, having never been in a police station. He was taken to an interrogation room, with a big mirror on one wall. He knew from TV shows that these mirrors were one-way, which allowed policemen to watch this room from a room on the other side.

When Hill and Vanzetti came into the room, Mike tried to explain. It came out in a rush, and sounded unconvincing, even to his own ears. He paced about the room, striving to succeed. Hill sat there, saying nothing, until Mike finished. There was an uncomfortable silence.

"Could you tell me where you were yesterday about noon, and this morning?" Hill said at last.

"Yesterday I was out doing errands. And this morning I was sleeping." Mike paused. "Why would you want to know about today?"

"Robert Sutter, also late of your firm, was killed by a hit-and-run driver this morning, as he was out jogging."

Mike was stunned into silence.

Hill looked at him. "The problem is, Mr. Morton, we haven't been able to find the old man you call rummy. But we know you did have grievances against the other men. You not only have a strong motive, you have no alibi at the times of these killings. We are going to charge you with these killings, Mr. Morton. I suggest you get a very good lawyer."

"This is crazy! The real killer is out there, and you want to lock me up! I couldn't kill anyone, I'm a successful businessman. Why are you doing this?"

"Take a look in the mirror, Mr. Morton," said Hill quietly.

When he looked up at the mirror, Mike was shocked to see an older, slovenly version of himself. With unwashed clothes that smelled of his last alcohol binge, and no shower or shave, he was someone you'd pass quickly on the street, wrinkling your nose in disgust. No one would hire a bum, a failure, who looked as bad as this. As he looked once more, his own watery, bloodshot eyes stared back at him. Then he caught a glimmer of a terrible smile, and began to sob.

THE PIT

I always thought my biggest fear in life was a cave-in. When you're working in a mine, with thousands of tons of earth above you, pressing down, that's how it is. You don't breathe easy until you're back up. You live in fear every time the support timbers creak. But then I discovered that down in the pit there are worse things to fear than a cave-in.

I'd worked in the mine for six years before the collapse, before all those men were murdered. Though I was still young, I looked a lot older. As we all did. You age fast down there, when you're always cramped, sweating, and trying to breathe while covered with coal dust.

We were working the night shift and waiting for the cage to take us down the shaft, when one of the company clerks brought over someone we hadn't seen before. "This here's Kovic," he said. "He'll be starting with you tonight." The clerk walked away, and left the stranger standing there.

We looked him over. He was thin and tall, and seemed more so, since he lacked the permanent stoop the rest of us had from working bent over all the time. He wore regular work clothes, but they were clean and new, the creases still in them. He had black hair underneath his miner's helmet, and the pale, white skin all of us night-shift miners had.

"Kovic is it?" said Jackson, the shift boss. "Ever mine coal before?"

"Yes," the stranger replied. He smiled. "In Europe. A long time ago."

We said nothing. Being down in the pit marks a man, and this man seemed unmarked.

"Europe," Jackson said. He spat out a stream of tobacco juice. "Nothin' personal, mister, but you look a mite consumptive to be down digging coal. We work a man's hard shift, and I need men who can fill those carts."

"I am quite healthy and fit for the work, I assure you," Kovic answered. He stuck out his hand, with the palm slightly up. "Care to try me?" He smiled.

Jackson smiled too, and took the proffered hand. Jackson was a big man, and stronger than any of us. The two men locked in a handshake test of strength, and after only a moment, we saw Jackson wince. He quietly said, "Okay," and Kovic released him. Jackson shook his hand and flexed it, shaking his head ruefully. The rest of us said nothing.

"Alright, no hard feelings," he said. "Just like to make sure every man on my shift pulls his weight. Do that and we'll get along fine. My name's Jackson, I'm shift boss here, and this is the rest of the crew."

We all nodded to Kovic, and wondered what he was doing here. The cage had come to take us down. The other crew came off, tired, dirty, unsmiling.

We rode down into Hell, past the strung lights, with the clanging racket of the generator in our ears. When we reached our level, we filed out. Every man got to his place, and we started in. Kovic wasn't too far from me, and the few times I happened to catch sight of him, he seemed to be doing okay. Either he really had mined before, or he got the hang of it pretty quick. He worked steadily, not stopping until break, just like the rest of us.

While we ate, we tried to find out a little about him, but he wasn't talkative. Most of us aren't the prying type, and if a man wants to be let alone, we don't press him. His way of talking and holding himself made us think he was educated, but it seemed to us like he was running away from something. We didn't mind, so long as he did his job, but we sure did wonder what would drive a man with learning to a dirty underground hole, where he can't even see daylight.

A few nights later, it was two hours into the shift when we felt everything around us shudder, like old Mother Earth was shrugging her shoulders. We dropped whatever we were doing and ran like fury toward the cage. Support timbers cracked, the sound of death. Tons of earth poured down the main shaft, and the lights went out. The sound of those crying out was lost in the crash of the earth settling around us, sealing us in.

We waited there, listening to the timbers in our section creak. The earth shook again. There was a loud crack near my head as the support gave way, and an avalanche of dirt knocked me flat. A support beam crushed my legs, and as the dirt began to cover me, I fought for consciousness, and lost.

I thought I heard someone calling me. I could see nothing, and couldn't tell where I was. Someone called my name again. Covered in dirt from my chest on down, I couldn't move. I groaned, and tasted dirt.

"Murphy!" someone called. "You still alive?"

"I guess so," I replied. "Can't move."

"Hold on, we'll come get you."

A beam of light from a helmet burned my eyes.

"Looks like we'll have to dig you out," the voice said.

"Legs," I said slowly. "I think my legs are broken."

"Damn," said the voice. "Give me a hand here, boys, let's get him out."

Several more lights joined the first one. Someone wiped the dirt off my face so I could breathe easier. I heard the sounds of digging. They were at it for awhile. I passed out again, woke up, and heard them talking.

"Timber right across his legs," someone said.

"Pretty lucky. Two more feet, and he'd be dead."

"Yeah, real lucky. Now he gets to die nice and slow with the rest of us."

"You just shut up with that kind of talk! Just shut up. We're not gonna die. They're going to get us out of here."

"Alright, we're not through here. Let's get him out. Slow and easy. Get that timber off him."

When they lifted the timber from my legs, the pressure was gone and the pain came flooding in. When they pulled me free, it was too much to bear.

I woke again and heard someone move beside me, coughing. There was a coat over me, and I could feel the pain searing through me.

"How ya doin'?" I recognized the voice, and the coughing, as Betters. He'd been in the pit for twenty years. Not even forty years old, and coughing his lungs out until he bled.

"Bad," I said feebly. "Hurts."

"Yeah, sorry," he said. "Ain't much we can do."

"Drink," I croaked.

"Drink? Sure thing." He was gone for a minute and was back.

"You take this real easy, now," he said. "Don't you let any of this spill. We don't have a lot, and we don't know how long we'll be down here."

"Okay," I said. The water in my mouth cut some of the coal dust and dirt away. It felt good.

"How bad is it?" I had to ask.

"Well, I won't lie to you," he coughed again. "Your legs are all busted up, you know that, and there's none of us down here knows how to set 'em, so you'll have to wait until they come for us. Can't help you none with the pain. We got some air, and the roof is shored up in our section here, so unless we get another rumble, we should be okay. We got a little water and some food. Should be enough to last until they dig down."

"Who made it?" I asked.

"Hansen, Jeffries, Pollack, O'Brien, you, me, and Kovic," he answered. I thought about the ones who hadn't had a chance, and said a silent prayer for them.

"How is everyone taking it?" I asked quietly.

28

"Okay, for the most part," he said. "Jeffries is a little shaky. Everyone else is pretty calm, even Kovic. Hey," he said cheerily. "It could be worse. We even have a couple of cigarettes."

"Bad for your lungs," I was glad to be able to crack the old joke. I guessed we were okay, considering. My legs were broken, sure, but there was nowhere to go if I'd been able to walk.

There was no sense of time passing down there in the dark. We were in limbo, waiting to see what our fate would be. Some of the men claimed to hear digging noises, but I couldn't tell if it was true or only wishful thinking. Not being able to move around, I would lay there and listen to the other men talk. I heard Jeffries arguing with the others. He sounded like he was cracking up. Betters coughed continually, and I could pick the others out when they spoke.

I clutched my mother's crucifix and tried to keep from sleeping and dreaming pain. I'd always gone to Mass on Sunday, our one day off, no matter how tired I was, because my Irish mother had brought me up that way. My father had gone, too, until he coughed his life away from the black lung. My mother didn't last long after he went, and I still wore her crucifix, to remind me of her. I missed her more than the old man. I'd rarely seen him, since he was mostly in the mine or sleeping when I was up. But every Sunday we were down at the church, praying for a better life, praying that nothing would happen to the men down under the ground.

The dreams that came to me were horrible, and I had trouble distinguishing between waking and dreaming. I kept feeling as if someone were watching me. Once I saw two red glowing eyes, and thought it was a rat. I felt as if they were watching me to see if I would die-a vulture, then. But there were no vultures down here. I tried to laugh and couldn't.

Then I felt the breath. It was warm and foul, as if something had rotted and died. I was disgusted and tried to block it out. The eyes moved closer and I sensed that whatever it was was larger than a rat. I moved my hand out and heard a hissing noise as something scrambled away from me.

I was bathed in sweat, but my mouth was dry. I fumbled for the canteen and finally found it. There wasn't much left in it as I heard the liquid sloshing around, but I took a small swig anyway. It helped some. I lay there awhile, thinking. I saw a light bob toward me as Betters came up.

"How you doing?" he asked.

"Okay, I guess," I said. "How's everyone holding out?"

"Jeffries is dead," Betters said flatly.

"Dead?" I said. "How?"

"Don't know. He was starting to get crazy awhile back. We got him calmed down some, and Hansen tripped over him awhile later. Heart must've given out." Betters coughed as a spasm seized him, and spat.

"Listen," I said quietly. "I saw something watching me, something with red eyes."

"Yeah, well, we've all had bad dreams."

"I don't think it was a dream," I said.

"Might've been a rat," Betters said. "You know we get 'em down here. Hell, we might be eating it before long."

"It was too big for a rat," I insisted.

"Yeah, well, you might have a bit of fever. Wouldn't be surprised."

"Maybe," I said. "But it scared me."

"We're all kind of scared right now," Betters said.

"How come nobody else is coming to talk to me?" I asked.

"Well, like I said, they're kind of scared," he said. "They figured if anybody wasn't gonna make it, it would be you, on account of your legs and all."

"Hey," I grabbed his arm. "I'm gonna make it."

"Yeah, sure, Murphy," he said.

"I'm gonna make it," I insisted. I tried to cling to Betters, but he released my hand from his arm. "I gotta go, Murphy. Be back in a little while."

I sank back, frightened. What if the others thought I was going to die and stopped giving me food and water? Would they just let me die like that? I held to the crucifix and prayed.

It was a while later before Betters came back.

"How ya doin?" he asked.

"Not so good," I admitted. "Betters, you guys won't cut me out of the food and water will you? Don't do that to me."

"Hey, you don't have to worry. If this keeps up, you'll have it all."

"What do you mean?" I asked.

"Pollack's dead."

"What? What the hell is going on?" I was scared.

"Don't know," he answered. "Thought it might be a gas leak, so we sniffed around pretty carefully. Maybe they just gave up."

"I'm not giving up," I said forcefully.

"That's good, Murphy," he said.

"How long we been down here?" I asked.

"Can't say. Two, three days, maybe."

"They'll come get us," I said.

"Sure, kid."

I awoke to sounds of shouting. Somebody was yelling, and somebody else was telling him to shut up. It cut off abruptly, but sounds still echoed down our corridor. Betters came by in a few minutes.

"What was that all about?" I said.

"Hansen was cursing everyone," Betters said. "We didn't mind at first, but he started getting louder and louder. He didn't quit until we told him he'd cause another cave-in. Then he went off into a corner and started muttering to himself."

31

"Is he gonna be alright?" I asked.

"Don't know," Betters replied. "I guess he's got a right to be spooked, but if he keeps it up, one of us is gonna bust him one to shut him up."

"How's the water and food holding up?" I said.

"We got a little left, not much. It's gonna be tough going if they don't get us soon. But hey, at least we still have air."

"Yeah."

I could hear Hansen when I drifted off to sleep again. There wasn't much else to do, stuck as I was in the dark and unable to move. I dreamed of open air, a field of wheat with a blue sky overhead. A breeze was blowing, and felt good on my face. I squinted and smiled up at the sun, all yellow and hot. My legs weren't broken, and I flexed them to feel the power in them. I began to run through the wheat, racing along with the wind. I laughed as I ran, and noticed a woman in a white dress with long yellow hair beckoning to me. I ran to embrace her, but heard a rumble and saw the ground open up before me. I fell, down into the earth, away from the sun and sky, and screamed as I went ever lower.

There was someone shaking me as I came out of the dream. His lamp was on, and shone into my face. For just a moment, I thought it was that friendly sun, but then I realized where I really was. I wanted to scream like in my dream. Instead I choked on my dry throat. A little water splashed into my mouth, and I got control.

"Betters?" I asked.

"Right here," he replied.

"Was I making noise?"

"Yeah, you were."

"I was having a dream," I told him. "I was on the surface, it was nice. Then the ground opened up, and I fell in."

"Well, we're still down here. And we got trouble. Kovic's a killer."

"What do you mean?" I asked.

"O'Brien's dead now," he answered. "Same as the others, no reason for it. That leaves Hansen, you and me. I give you the benefit of the doubt. Hansen's gone off the deep end, and I know I didn't do it. So that leaves Kovic."

"How do you know?" I said.

"Three men dead, one at a time. Took the light over them, but can't tell. I know they were killed, though. Kovic did it."

"How did he do it?" I asked "Poison?"

"Nah," he replied, after a moment's thought. "We all drank from the same canteens and shared the same food. I don't know how he did it, but he sure was quiet. We never heard any of 'em go."

"What about Hansen?" I said. "Couldn't he have done it? You said he's acting crazy."

"No, he was right by me, muttering away. I would have noticed. Besides, Kovic moved further down the shaft. He knows I know it's him. What he don't know is, I got a knife. When he comes for me, I'm gonna stick him."

"Why's he doing it?" I said.

"I dunno," Betters replied. "Maybe that's why he came here in the first place, cause he done something like that somewhere else and was running away."

"What are you going to do?" I asked.

"He can't sneak up on both of us," Betters said. "I'd bring Hansen over, but every time I get near him, he pulls away. But you and me will stay here and take turns looking out."

We talked for awhile, and alternately listened, but heard only the sound of Hansen mumbling, only a few feet away. When I began to get sleepy, Betters said he was too keyed up to sleep, so he'd keep watch. He had his knife out, resting it on his leg as he sat with his back to the wall. I drifted off, listening to one man who coughed, one man who prayed, and one man who stayed ominously quiet.

I came to and realized something was wrong. I listened for a minute, and could not hear Betters. The coughing had become such a comforting thing, since I could always tell where he was, but now it was gone. I yelled his name and listened to my own echo. I yelled again and heard Hansen muttering to himself. I was now left with only a madman and a murderer for company.

My worst predicament was that I could not find the canteen that had been by my side. Hansen had to have some, but he was yards away, nothing for a healthy man but as good as miles to me. Calling to Hansen over and over did no good. I would have to crawl over and steal some water.

Rolling over, I felt the first flash of pain. As I dragged myself along the floor, every gain in ground was matched by agony. It took a long time, and I passed out at least twice. Mining coal now seemed easy compared to this.

After what seemed like a hundred years I made it over to where Hansen sat against the wall. He still refused to acknowledge me, and kept mumbling. I felt around in the dark for a long time, until my fingers closed over the strap of a canteen. Pulling it to me, I heard a sloshing, promising liquid inside.

A light suddenly blinded me, and I yelled in pain and surprise. Hansen grabbed the canteen from me and moved away. He was so far gone he wouldn't even let me have water. If I made it over to his new location, he would move again. I was lost, and wept in despair. I almost hoped Kovic would kill him and leave me the canteen.

The hours dragged slowly. The pain kept me awake for awhile, but finally settled into a dull ache. When I awoke, I could no longer hear Hansen muttering. Kovic had got him as well, leaving me as the last and most powerless victim. I was at the point where I hardly cared. If they didn't dig through to us shortly, nothing would matter anyway.

I was at the point where my hunger and thirst were competing for attention, when I felt the presence. Somehow it was still enough to frighten me.

"Kovic?" I called, my voice cracked.

"Yes," he answered. "I am here."

"Why did you do it? Why kill us all?"

"I was hungry," he replied.

"But you didn't..."

"Eat them?" he chuckled. The sound chilled me. "No, nothing like that. I just needed their blood."

"Blood?" I said, shocked. "What for?"

"It is what I need for nourishment."

"What are you talking about?" I said.

"Mr. Murphy, surely you're not as unschooled as that?" he said. "You must have heard legends or folklore about such as I."

I thought for a minute, and it hit me. I was glad it was dark and he couldn't see my face.

"Oh my God," I said, very afraid. "It can't be true."

"I assure you, Mr. Murphy, it is quite true. I am not a product of your fevered imagination."

"Why did you come here?" I asked.

"Circumstances," he sighed. "Certain people have been after me for some time. I find it tiresome to keep on the move, so I came here for a rest. This accident, though, has changed matters somewhat."

"You came to a coal mine for a rest?" I said.

"Certainly," he replied. "The labor, so burdensome to you, is of no consequence to me. Since we work at night, I never have to endure the sunlight, and no one would disturb a poor tired sleeping miner in the day. My skin pallor blends in with everyone else's, and here I can remain anonymous, with no embarrassing questions. Also, I actually was a miner, a long time ago. I am rather surprised that conditions have not changed much in almost a hundred years."

"This is too much," I said, not wanting to believe.

"Believe what you will. Your companions didn't even know what was happening, even as I drained their life's blood."

"Why save me for last?" I said.

"Sheer accident," he stated. "In fact, you were supposed to be first, since no one expected you to live. I thought to harvest you while you were still fresh."

"That was you!" I said. "That time I woke up, it was you watching me."

"That is true. You were saved temporarily by your little amulet."

"My cross," I said, reaching for it to hold it tight.

"Yes," he said with seeming distaste. "But now you have a quandary, Mr. Murphy. You have no food and no water. Without it you will not last for very much longer. I will make you a deal. I will give you the water you so desperately need, and even all the food left, and you will be able to live a little while longer."

"Before you kill me," I said bitterly.

"But at least you will die painlessly, and not in horrible agony. Have you seen men die of thirst, Mr. Murphy? I have, and it is not pretty at all. Tongues blackened and swollen, eyes wide with suffering. This fate awaits you. Or you can have your fill of water and food, and when you are asleep, the end will come swiftly and painlessly. I offer you mercy."

"Some mercy," I said.

"Oh, come now," he said. "Did you hear the others as they went? No. You won't even know what's happening. Your end is inevitable, Mr. Murphy. How you die depends solely upon you. Swift and painless or a long drawn-out suffering. Water and mercy for you to throw away a piece of useless jewelry. What do you say?"

"I say go to hell," I replied.

"You are a fool," he hissed. "Very well, Mr. Murphy, enjoy your suffering." I heard him move away, and then I was alone.

My mouth ached for liquid. I ran a fever, and wondered if this was what dying was like. I could no longer feel my body, except when I clutched the cross, which gave me strength.

I thought a lot about dying, and what had brought me here. I dreamed of when I was a young boy, watching the older men go off to the mines, wondering when it would be my turn. Everyone had that stooped, haggard look, but when my turn came, I went willingly. When you're born in a mining town you can't imagine anything else. I realized that it wasn't any kind of a life, that you just wore yourself out making money for someone else. One day you started coughing like Betters, then later they put you in a box.

Gurgling water coursed through my dreams. I awoke and sensed Kovic near. He was shaking a canteen, taunting me.

"Do you hear that, Mr. Murphy?" he called to me. "Clear, sweet water. All you want can be yours. Remove that thing from around your neck while you still have the strength."

The sound of the water made me mad with desire. I wanted it worse than anything else in my life, but I knew I couldn't. I squeezed the cross in my hand until it hurt, and that helped take my mind off my thirst. I wanted to curse him, but I couldn't make my dry throat work, and I had no water even for tears. I lay there knowing I was going to die, but at least I wouldn't be food for Kovic.

While dreaming again, I heard a scratching in the earth. I thought it was rats coming to get me, all of them with long white teeth, and many of them with Kovic's face. I saw a glimmer of light and thought I had died. Voices came to me, the voices of the dead, I thought. Something touched my face, and then I was floating. There were more voices, and a breeze.

Later, I felt my head laying on something soft. My legs hurt again, but they felt far away. My hand brushed something that felt like a sheet. Death sure was strange. Light came through my eyelids, and I opened my eyes, to find myself in a room. It took a minute to realize I wasn't dead. When I turned my head, a woman sitting in a chair stood up and left the room. A man came and stood next to me. Tears streamed down my face as I looked up.

"You're okay now," the man said. "Rest now." I understood that he was a doctor.

In the days that followed, my mind and body healed. Rescue teams had finally dug through the section of tunnel where we were stranded, and they said I was the only one they found alive. I was almost dead, but after the fever broke, they reset my legs and put in metal pins to strengthen them.

They never found Kovic. He must have hid and then come up later, when it was dark. I said that he'd murdered them all, but didn't say anything else. They'd have claimed I was crazy from being down there too long and put me away. I wasn't sure myself how much was real and how much I hallucinated. Trying to think of it now, there are pieces missing, like I'm trying to remember someone else's life and it's not all there.

Not being able to go back in the mines was a blessing. I left the town where I was born and raised and spent the next thirty years doing better than just working in a pit until I dropped. Chicago is a mighty big place after a mining town. I'm married and have children, and go to Mass every Sunday. My wife, my children, and I have one unbreakable habit. Each of us wears around our neck a silver cross, at all times.

For thirty years, I've thought the past was dead and buried, like so many of the men I grew up with. But last night my wife took me to an opera downtown. And I saw him. Thirty years, and he looks the same. Dressed in evening clothes instead of miner's wear, I still recognized him. He didn't see me, at least I hope he didn't. Because now I have to hunt him down, and kill him somehow, for all the men he killed. But I'm afraid, so very afraid. I could tell people, but they'd say I was crazy, so I guess I'm alone in this.

Tonight I'll go to where I think he is. I feel like the cage has come for me, and I'm going back down into the pit.

CARNIVAL OF PAIN

The Carnival was coming to town, and just by looking at the poster, Billy Bonney knew it was going to be something special. The colors in the illustrations were bright, almost glowing, but he noticed the way they were combined was somehow unsettling if you looked at them too long.

Billy gazed with wonder and a keen yearning at the enticements and promised attractions. Exotic characters beckoned to him: Strong Man Samson, Rondo, the Human Rubber Band, Fiero the Fire-Eater, Electro-Girl, Mysteria the Fortuneteller, Kackles the Clown, and more. There were rides advertised, too, like the Drop of Death, the Wheel of Wonder, the Crackback Coaster. Excitement and the hint of danger. And as a truly different touch, the carnival was only open at night.

Billy reached out to touch the poster. The paper was glossy and felt unpleasantly slick, and he drew his hand away. He looked at the headline, The Carnival of Pan. It was outlined in a special way that made Pan kind of look like Pain. Cool. A carnival of pain sounded really dangerous. This was going to be some adventure, and Billy had been rather short on that in his life so far.

Billy's mind was racing. How could he see the carnival? He had to come up with a plan. Since Billy's father had skipped out of the family picture, Billy's mom was stuck working two jobs to pay all the bills and take care of him. So there was no money for extras, like admission tickets, and his mom would not be able to get time off from work to take him. Same reason he'd had to leave Scouts. He was too young to have a job, and had no money of his own, so he'd have to find some way to get there and get in.

Billy wouldn't mind working for his admission, but he doubted they'd accept his labor. If only he were older. As to getting there physically, it was only a few miles, so he could get there on his bike. Sure, it would have to be at night, but Billy knew all the paths in this town so well, he was positive he could navigate there in the dark.

Seven days until the carnival opened. It was the longest week of Billy's life.

Finally, opening day arrived, and Billy was ready. He had carefully mapped out his route. He had squirreled away a flashlight, and when the time came, would strap it to the front of the bike with duct tape, as a homemade headlight. He had his Boy Scout jackknife, and dark clothes for nighttime prowling. He ate a hearty dinner with his mother, did the dishes, and said goodbye to her as she went off to work. As soon as he was sure she was gone, he put on the dark clothes, gathered his things, and went out to his bike.

Mounted atop his trusty steed, Billy rode through the night, his lone, bouncing beam of light slicing a narrow, feeble path for him through the dark. He avoided busy roads and houses with dogs, took four shortcuts where he had to walk his bike, and so arrived at the carnival without incident.

Billy parked his bike in the woods and studied the layout of the carnival grounds. There was a high wire fence around the whole thing, so it looked like they were quite serious about making everyone pay to get in through the front gate. He saw a few people doing so.

Various rides poked metal arms up over the fence, brightly lit with people strapped into the seats. Billy heard screams and loud cries within the grounds, but was surprised to hear no laughter.

Billy scanned the length of the fence that he could see, and saw no security guards. There were no lights shining on the fence either, so it was evident they thought the presence of the fence alone would deter anyone from sneaking in. He left the cover of the woods and reached the fence, at the back end furthest from the entrance.

Billy walked along the fence, testing it for weaknesses. He found a spot where the wire bowed out a bit, on an uneven patch of ground. By pulling on the bottom of the fence, he made a bigger space between ground and wire. He dug with determined focus for over ten minutes, scooping out loose soil with his hands. He didn't worry too much about getting dirty. He did his own laundry, so his mother wouldn't see it, and perhaps the night and the dark clothes would hide the dirt enough while he was at the carnival. He felt a little guilty about sneaking in, but convinced himself he had no choice.

Finally, Billy felt there was enough of a space for him to slip through underneath. He eased himself under, bit by bit, careful not to snag his clothes on the pronged ends of the fence wire. He felt like a prisoner of war making an escape, like he'd seen in an old movie once, but he was breaking in, not out.

And finally he was through. Had he been any bigger, he wouldn't have made it, so for once his size was an asset.

He stood up and looked around to see if he had been noticed, but saw no one. He made his way to the closest structures and walked between them, out onto to the broad path of the carnival midway.

The sights, smells, and sounds flooded his senses. There were ringing bells, the clack of the metal legs of the rides as they went through their motions, and from somewhere, a megaphoned exhortation to a sideshow. There were bright lights, people, and movement. Billy gazed around, taking it all in.

But something was wrong. There were no smiles on the people as they milled about. Their faces were fearful and contorted, as though they were being hurt in some fashion. Billy looked closer, and thought he saw something on a woman's shoulder, some shape at the back of her neck. He looked at someone else, and they had it as well. A small, indistinct lump, dark and ominous. Billy checked every person he saw, and everyone had one. Men, women, children, everyone. Everyone but him.

Uneasy now, Billy moved along the side of the path, toward the main gate. Perhaps he should tell someone, see if they could do something, or at least tell him what was going on. But then again, they might guess that he got in without paying, and he could be in trouble. So he would just keep out of sight until he figured out what to do.

To avoid being seen, Billy slipped into the back of a tent along the midway. He heard a harsh, accented voice speaking behind a curtain. He peeked through a slit and saw an older woman in a head kerchief, gold earring and flowing Gypsy garb, seated at a table which held a crystal ball. This must be Mysteria the Fortuneteller. Across from her was a much younger woman, who was crying. Billy could see that the crying woman had one of the mysterious lumps on her shoulder, but the fortuneteller did not. The younger woman seemed to stagger as she got to her feet, and stumbled out the front. The fortuneteller smiled.

An older man made a hesitant entrance, and the fortuneteller beckoned him forth and gestured to the empty chair. The man sat, and asked a question in a voice so low that Billy could not hear it. Billy could see that the man had his own lump on his shoulder, and it seemed to be moving.

The fortuneteller hunched over her crystal and murmured to herself. She began to speak, and told the man terrible things that she said she had seen in his future. His business would fail, his family would desert him, and he would be destitute and homeless within the year. The man looked stricken, and got to his feet. He swayed a bit, but managed to stumble out of the tent.

Billy had had enough. He left, intending to slip back out the way he had come. But a crowd had gathered in that direction, herding to watch at a barker's call to see Samson, the World's Strongest Man. A large man in a leopard-print tunic that strapped over one shoulder was hefting a barbell with enormous weights on each end. The people stood still to watch, and Billy noted the lump on each person's shoulder, all except the barker and the strong man on the stage.

The barker called for a volunteer from the audience, and pointed to a man in the crowd. The man, who was large and strong-looking himself, came forth, seemingly dazed, but got up on the stage with the strong man, who handed him a smaller barbell, with only one weight on each end. The man could not sustain the weight, however, and it crashed to the flooring. Everyone laughed, and the barker made cutting remarks about how weak the man was. To drive home the point, Samson picked up the barbell easily with one hand, and the crowd laughed again. The volunteer now stood red-faced, and tears seemed ready to burst from his eyes. The barker continued to taunt him as he went back down into the crowd, and the barker called for another volunteer.

Billy did not stay to watch, but walked in the other direction. When he reached the front gate, he saw that the carnival people had set up a maze, so that people walking in had to turn a corner, and were out of sight of people behind them. As they passed a certain point, a man with slicked-back white hair placed a small, furry, ball-like thing on the back of each person's neck. The person stiffened when this happened, as if the thing had bitten into them. Billy also saw their eyes change, and if they had been laughing or talking, they stopped suddenly.

"Hello, little boy," came a voice from behind Billy. He turned quickly, and saw a hideous-looking clown in a green

43

outfit, with bright orange hair, coming towards him. He looked closer, and saw that the clown's eyes were silver, like pools of mercury. Billy opened his mouth, but no sound came out.

"Aren't you a bad little boy?" The clown's voice was a harsh croak. "Got in without paying the price? We'll fix that."

A soiled, white-gloved hand reached for Billy, who caught a horrible scent from the clown, of whiskey, and sweat, and worse things. It sparked him to run, and he slipped from the grasp of the foul clown. He darted in among the tents as a cry went up behind him.

Billy had to hide, and he slipped into one of the tents that was dark inside. He fumbled about in the dark, trying to be quiet.

"Who's there?" came a soft voice, and suddenly there was a light blue glow in the interior of the tent. Billy saw a young girl in a cage, and she was the source of the light. He turned to run.

"Wait," said the girl. "I'm not one of them."

Billy turned back. The dark-haired girl wore a long black dress with long, ragged sleeves, and had a curious look on her face.

"I know what you're thinking," she said. "That we're all monsters here. Most are, because of those things they put on, the harmlings. But I don't have one."

"They didn't, either," Billy said, surprised to hear his own.

"They do," the girl said. "But after the harmlings feed for awhile, they get smaller, so small you can't notice them. They feed on pain, and they eat very well here. But they can't stay on me, because I'm the Electric Girl." She held up her hand, and a tiny sizzle of blue sparked out.

"You don't have a carnival name?" said Billy.

"They won't give me one, because I'm not one of them. That's why they keep me in here." She indicated the bars of her cage.

"What about your own name?"

"Audra Lee," the girl said. "I haven't told anyone that in a long time."

"I'm Billy."

"How come you don't have a harmling?"

"I didn't have any money, so I got in through a hole in the fence in back."

"Billy, you've got to get away. If they catch you, they put a harmling on you, and it's terrible. It destroys people."

"What about you? We can escape together."

"The key is over there," the girl pointed to a wall of the tent.

From outside, they heard voices coming towards them.

"Hide in that chest," the girl pointed to a stout wooden chest with iron straps that sat nearby. "Hurry."

With no other choice, Billy did as she said. He lifted the lid and jumped in, landing atop a pile of carnival costumes. He pulled the lid shut on top of him. He heard the voice of the horrible clown.

"You, girl, did you see a boy run through here?"

"I didn't see anyone."

"If you're lying, you won't see anything ever again."

Billy crouched inside, trembling and fearful, until he hear the girl whisper.

"You can come out now."

Billy pushed back the lid and leaped out. He ran to the hanging ring of keys, and brought it back to the lock of the cage. The girl pointed to one of the keys on the ring.

"That one."

Billy put the key into the lock and turned. There was a click, and the lock came free. He opened the door of the cage, and the girl stepped out and hugged him. Billy was completely embarrassed, never having been hugged by a girl before. But it felt good.

"Thank you," she whispered. "I've been in there a long time."

"How do we get out of here?" Billy said.

"They'll have the whole place locked up tight. There's too many of them. We'll need to create a diversion."

"How?"

The girl hurried over to a cabinet and opened it. Inside were bottles. She took some down and handed four to Billy.

"What's this?" Billy said. There was liquid inside each.

"Alcohol," the girl replied. "They drink a lot here, all of them. But it'll burn. Smash the bottles along the edge of the tent."

Billy watched as the girl hurled several bottle to the ground, breaking them open. He understood, and did the same. He watched as she broke the neck off another bottle, and splashed the contents along the fabric walls. He followed suit, and when his bottle was empty, he tossed it aside.

He saw her pull on a cloth, and it fell off to reveal a bank of cages with several dozen of the small, furry lumps.

"The harmlings," she said, and splashed more of the alcohol over the cages and animals. They hissed and lunged at the bars of their cages, snapping sharp-looking teeth in frustration.

"We need more," she said, and Billy started for the cabinet to get more bottles. But he heard the voice of the clown.

"Gotcha."

Billy turned around to see the arms of the clown around the girl. She fought back, but the clown passed her to Samson, the World's Strongest Man, who held her tightly.

A few of the others came inside, blocking off any escape. There was the white-haired man from the gate, a dark, bald man in a blue outfit, the fortuneteller, and a tall, skinny man.

"Give it up, kid," the clown said. "Come get your medicine." The clown walked to the harmling cages.

Desperate, Billy pulled out his jackknife and opened the blade, holding it out before him. The clown laughed and snapped his fingers.

"You're scaring me, kid. Fiero, scorch him a little, teach him a lesson."

Billy saw the bald man in blue take a deep breath. He remembered the name from the poster, and knew what was coming. Sure enough, spurt of flame shot from the man's mouth, and Billy jumped aside. The flame hit some of the spilled alcohol, which ignited with a whoosh. The whole interior of the tent popped into a roomful of flame.

Billy heard a scream, and saw the strong man's face contort in pain. The girl broke free of his grip, wreathed in blue waves of lightning. There were more screams, as the outfits of some of the performers caught fire.

Billy reached for the girl with his free hand, and ran to one section of the tent wall that wasn't yet enveloped in flame. He stuck the knife in the fabric and slashed down, opening a slit. More air rushed in to feed the flames, and the inside of the tent was all fire as Billy and the Electric Girl ducked through the slit to the outside and started running.

"What do we do now?" Billy yelled.

"We have to get some help," she said. Crowds of people stood dumbly, watching the flaming bonfire of a tent, with flames spreading on all sides. She went up and reached out with her finger to touch a lump on one man's neck. A spark of blue shot out, and the harmling fell to the ground, where Billy stomped it before it could scuttle off. The man rubbed his face as if waking from a bad dream.

The girl was touching other harmlings, and Billy was trying to keep up, squashing each one underfoot as they fell. People started shouting to each other, aware of the danger now and rousing others. After relieving a few dozen more, the girl turned to Billy.

"That's enough. They'll realize what happened, see the others and take care of it. Let's get out of here."

Billy lead her to the back of the carnival as the night was alive with walls of fire. They got to the fence and skittered under, helping each other as the fence prongs tried to scratch at them. And then they were free, and outside of the burning carnival.

"What now?" said Billy.

"I have to go," said the girl. "But I'll be back. When you've grown up." She paused. "You were very brave, you know, and you saved me. I'll never forget that."

The she wrapped her arms around Billy's neck and kissed him. It was a strange feeling, and he almost jumped away, but let himself be drawn into it. She let go and walked away, smiling over her shoulder.

Billy's lips still tingled, and he waved as his first love walked away in the dark. He hoped she'd come back, as she'd said, and he couldn't wait to grow up.

LOCUST TIME

Seventeen years has passed, and it's time for the locusts to return. They will emerge from the ground, after having lain dormant for so long. They are actually cicadas, but to me they're locusts, like the plague mentioned in the Bible, and they plague me with memories. For when they were last here, my darling Jenny died.

It was Jenny who first told me about the locusts and their strange ways. It was the beginning of the summer, and she was still vibrant and alive. The sun highlighted her blond hair and brown, healthy skin. Her eyes sparkled green and bright, like new bits of glass found on the beach. She was like the ocean, gentle as rolling waves, but wide and deep and capable of anything.

Jenny and I were at the beach one day after school of our senior year, enjoying the quiet before the summer crowds came. We sat on the pier and pitched seashells into the water. She loved to collect pretty shells on our walks along the beach, and then throw them back into the sea after admiring them. We would talk while we did this, and since Jenny read a lot, she was always coming up with interesting things to discuss.

Usually I enjoyed talking about whatever she mentioned, but that day she told me about the seventeen-year locusts. She told me how they lay underground, not dead, but always waiting to come back. Though the day was bright and sunny, I felt chilled. I always hated insects, and this talk was worse, for these locusts seemed like some kind of vampire. They were unnatural, with their alien bodies and black, cold eyes. I wondered what evil dreams they had, waiting down there in the dark earth.

When I told Jenny how I felt, she laughed at my fears. She dumped the rest of her seashells down the front of my T-shirt, then leaped up and ran down the shore. I howled in surprise at the cold, wet feeling of the shells, gritty with sand, against my skin.

Jumping to my feet, I pulled out my shirt and brushed with both hands to rid myself of my most unwelcome burden. I chased Jenny down the beach, though I knew full well she could easily escape, given her head start and those long, brown legs of hers. But she stopped and turned, doubled over with laughter to see me running so furiously after her. When I caught her, I wrestled her out into the surf so I could dunk her. I managed to get her head under, but she slipped away, laughing. She was always slipping away.

By now, we were both out of breath. We waded onto the shore and sat in the wet sand, waves playfully nudging us as we gazed out over the ocean. I turned to look at Jenny, and she cocked her head and looked back at me. One side of her mouth pulled up in that special smile of hers, the one I knew so well. Her hair hung like seaweed, stringy and tangled from the saltwater, but still she was beautiful. I told her I loved her and kissed her for the first time. She didn't say anything, and I thought it was because she felt the same way. I should have known better. Maybe if she'd spoken truthfully to me then, things would have worked out differently.

After she told me about the locusts, I couldn't stand any insects buzzing around me. But it was summertime, and they were everywhere. I decided to wage war on them, and kill as many as I could. I wasn't sure now that they would stay dead, but I killed them anyway.

One day when I wasn't working at my father's garage, I got a big glass jar and put some gasoline in it. Then I got a smaller jar, and went out around the house, catching whatever insects I could. One by one, I'd bring them back and drop them into the big killing jar. They couldn't escape, and I liked that. There would be no coming back. They'd kick and buzz for awhile, but the gasoline did the trick. When I had too many bodies floating in the big jar, I emptied it out, started a controlled fire with their gas-soaked bodies, and started over. I did this so much I heard buzzing in my head, and I didn't sleep so well for awhile, until I got used to it.

Jenny kept teasing me about the locusts. She visited me when I was working at the garage, and she said that cars reminded her of insects. The engines were just like buzzing, the painted exteriors were hard, shiny shells, and headlights were huge round eyes.

I hated to hear her talk like that, and asked her to stop, but she kept it up, making buzzing noises and pinching me. I got scared and kind of slapped her, the way you'd smack a bug. She got mad, and I apologized, but the damage was done. She didn't talk to me for a week.

I saw her walking home after dark one night, and asked her if she'd like a ride. She said she wouldn't, but I apologized some more, and she finally got in. I drove out to a quiet spot, on the hills overlooking town. She smiled like she knew I was going to go there.

I stopped the car and told her how sorry I was about what had happened, and that I really loved her. She laughed and said fine, but could I please drive her home now. I asked her how she felt about me. She said she thought I was okay, but she was going on vacation with her folks soon and leaving for college when she returned. She didn't see much point in our going out any more, but she would write me from college.

I couldn't believe what I was hearing. All the time we had spent together, all the years we had known each other, and now this. I asked her if she had ever loved me, and she said not really. I called her a liar, and her face twisted up like she'd eaten something disagreeable. She asked me coldly if I would take her home at once.

Everything was falling apart, and nothing I could say would change her mind. I was losing the only thing in life that mattered. There was a buzzing sound, as if a swarm of locusts were in my head. The next thing I knew, I took out a heavy flashlight and was holding it in my hand. Jenny opened the car door to get out, and I don't remember anything else for a while after that.

When I came to, I was crying, but I couldn't remember why. I sat in the car and held Jenny in my arms. All the warmth had left her, and that wasn't right. She was always so warm. There was some blood around, and I realized what had happened, and what I had to do. I put Jenny in the trunk of my car, and drove home.

My folks still weren't back, so I got a shovel from the shed and a blanket from inside the house. I wrapped the blanket around Jenny, a bright plaid thing we never used.

Under our house was a short tunnel, created as a fallout shelter by my grandfather, back when they thought the Russians would someday drop atomic bombs on us. It was never used, and no one in town knew we had it. We never used it for anything either, and had sealed it up years before.

It was a simple matter to open up the tunnel. I took Jenny and the shovel and flashlight, and went down the passage. When I found a good spot, I went to work with the shovel. I left Jenny there, and sealed the tunnel up again afterward.

The police questioned a lot of people about Jenny's disappearance, but they didn't get anywhere, and eventually gave it up. It became the big mystery of the town, and was assumed she'd run off.

I continued to work at the garage, until my father got too old to manage it. We both realized that I couldn't run it without him, so he sold it. I had no desire to leave by then, so I took care of him and my mother, until each passed in turn. I had no brothers or sisters, and so finally had the house to myself.

But I began to make some changes. I knew the locusts would be coming back, so I came up with a plan. If I got everything just right, I wouldn't have to go outside when they returned. I wouldn't have to feel their bodies crunching underfoot, see them devour everything outside, feel their foul touch as they brushed against me.

It took several years, but I was finally ready. New siding sheathed the outside in metal. All the window frames were replaced with new ones, and over those were storm shutters, solid and airtight. The chimney was sealed shut by a specialist. All cracks, crevices, and openings were painstakingly covered over, until there was no way for a locust to get inside. I would be safe.

Downstairs in the cellar was a generator, a big spare freezer, and an extra refrigerator. I had bought huge amounts of everything I would need from one of those big warehouse clubs. I stacked them on the shelves my grandfather had installed, waiting for a war that never came. When my war came, I would be ready.

And now it's locust time again. When it began, I sealed off the last passages to the outside. Nothing could get in or out. I had music to shut out the sound of the buzzing. I had no television, so as not to see them on the news, pouring forth from the ground and covering everything. I know they're out there, but if I can't see them or hear them, they won't bother me. Let them fly in their hideous swarms and cover the ground, the trees, and every building, eating away at every living thing. I'm in here, safe and quiet.

What I didn't count on was Jenny speaking to me in my dreams. She tells me she's coming back, after seventeen years. She says that she has learned the secret of the locusts, and is returning with them.

And tonight I heard something from downstairs. It almost sounded like someone softly calling my name. I knew I was just hearing things, and turned the music up louder.

When the power went out, I sat in the dark for a time, but that was unbearable. I'd have to go down and start the generator. Fear overwhelmed me, though I kept telling myself there was no reason to be afraid. I took the flashlight and went down the stairs.

I went to the entrance to the bomb shelter, and saw that it had been opened. There was a powerful odor of something that had lain too long underground. It was strong and noxious, and my knees were trembling. I heard a rustling sound, like dry cornstalks being rubbed together.

Something was in the shadows, over by the shelves. I turned and flashed the light on it. I saw the rotted remains of a plaid blanket, and there was a shape covered in dirt, with brown, wrinkled skin. Whatever it was stared at me with black, soulless eyes. I thought at first it was some giant locust, but it called my name, and I realized it was Jenny. I screamed and ran up the stairs. I dropped the flashlight, but could not stop to retrieve it. Stumbling around, I bumped into furniture and caromed off a wall, falling back on the floor.

Dazed for a moment, I could hear the locusts outside. They seemed to be waiting. The clackings and clickings as they rubbed their limbs in anticipation of the meals to come filled the air around the house with a maddening regularity. In my mind's eye, I could see their thousands as they filled the trees and shrubs, covered the house, littered the ground, until there was no place to walk without crunching one sickeningly underfoot. They were hungry, and all around, other swarms leapt from the ground and into the sky, obscuring the moon like drifting clouds. Their wings beating impossibly loud could drive a man mad.

With scraping sounds from the cellar coming closer, I imagined the Jenny-thing crossing the linoleum. Desperately, I heaved to my feet and threw myself against the back door. And that's when the true horror struck me: there was to be no escape. I had been too efficient, and never planned on getting out of the house in any kind of a hurry. With madness tearing at my mind, I tore my hands bloody trying to get hold of the planks that I'd nailed across the doorway. At my heels, I heard the Jenny-thing dragging itself toward me, imagined the ghostly touch of its limbs on my shoulders. It was then that I heard somebody scream, and with a noise that filled the air with thunder, the locusts outside heaved into the sky with a deafening roar.

Dale T. Phillips

THE LAST BATTLE

It seemed to Duval as if they had been marching for a thousand years. The sun beat down with a blistering heat as the patrol of French Regular Army soldiers made their way through the Vietnamese landscape. No one talked in the oppressive heat, not even for their favorite pastime of cursing the paratroopers of the Legion. Corporal Duval was sunburned and chafed from the long walk, and to amuse himself, thought up creative ways of killing the colonel who had sent them on this mission.

Duval looked up at the lieutenant, wondering when the man would call for a rest. He knew the lieutenant, an effete Parisian playboy in civilian life, couldn't last much longer. The lieutenant had joined the army because he had fed on romantic visions, and because he looked quite dashing in the uniform. Once in the service, he had realized his dreadful mistake. He now hoped for something heroic and not too sacrificial, perhaps a slight wound received while performing some act of unmitigated bravery. Enough for a medal or two before returning to the women of Paris and a life of comfortable uselessness.

The tired men would certainly get no rest from the sergeant. A petty criminal from the docks of Marseilles, he had killed two German soldiers just before the end of the last war. Though he shot them in the back when they tried to search his truckload of black-market goods, war made him a patriot and a hero. A vicious, street-tough brute, he was hated but feared by all the men in the patrol.

The enlisted men were a mixed lot. The French Army had taught them how to hold, clean, and fire a rifle, and how to march. None of them cared about the doomed French effort to cling to its colony. They were contemptuous of the locals, to them a strange, barbaric, little people, who only seemed to care about the rice crop which kept them alive.

Duval was the exception, the one who did not look down upon the people whose land they had invaded. He had even learned to speak Vietnamese. For that they made him a corporal. He came from a proud old military family who traced their ancestors back to the Normans of William the Conqueror. His father, older brother, and uncles had all fought in the Resistance, and he had missed out by being too young. Now he was taking his place in the family destiny, and hating every minute of it.

While the sergeant scouted ahead, the rest of the patrol shambled in a loose, undisciplined line. They sloshed through a rice paddy, passing a farmer with a water buffalo.

Duval reached down to pull a leech from his leg. He mopped perspiration from his face and shrugged his shoulders against the weight of the field pack. He wondered if all the wars his ancestors had fought in were this hard and filthy. His sweat-soaked clothing clung to him. He reached down to pull the shirt away from his skin, and was surprised when his fingers closed around something other than wet fabric. He looked down and saw small, interlocking metal rings where his shirt should be. Duval closed his eyes and shook his head. He reached down again, and felt the reassuring soggy army cloth. He wondered if the sun was getting to him, and took a long pull from his canteen.

They left the open ground and entered the jungle. Several of the men halfheartedly hacked a path through the jungle growth, following the trail of the sergeant. Duval swiped weakly at a vine and looked up at Moreau in front of him. Moreau was wearing some kind of leather armor, his bayonet was too long, and his helmet was now an odd shape. The landscape flickered and changed, showing trees that didn't belong in the jungle. Duval stumbled over a root, caught himself, and looked up once more. Things were back to normal.

Duval felt his forehead, but couldn't tell if he had a fever. He mentally reviewed what he knew of tropical diseases that caused hallucinations.

The lieutenant finally signaled a halt, and the men gratefully slumped to the ground, after first checking for snakes and booby traps. As the men sucked noisily from their canteens, Duval walked over to his superior, who sat a short distance away from the men.

"Lieutenant," he said quietly. The man looked up, exhaustion showing on his face.

"I think I have a fever. I'm seeing things."

"What things?"

Duval noticed Moreau staring at him. He shifted his weight, feeling foolish and uncomfortable.

"Odd things. Like strange trees. And Moreau holding a long machete or a sword."

"Go sit down," the lieutenant said wearily. "It's too hot."

Duval shrugged and walked away. He sat down and took a drink from his canteen. He smelled a strange scent, and sniffed the opening of the canteen, but it wasn't the water. He heard a whinny and recognized the smell of horses. What was happening? There were no horses in this part of Vietnam. He looked around to see if anyone else had heard it.

Only Moreau returned his gaze, eyes wide. He crawled on over to Duval. "You been seeing things, huh?" he asked.

Duval nodded.

Moreau looked around and licked his lips. "I been seeing some things too," he confided in a low voice.

"Why didn't you say something?"

"What good is it going to do?" Moreau shrugged. "He won't do anything," he nodded in the direction of the lieutenant. "And it'll just get us in trouble. That cochon of a sergeant would think we're playing sick and kick our ass."

"What did you see?" asked Duval.

"What you said. The trees were different, not like the jungle here. And I had a sword, and was wearing a kind of leather coat. It was weird."

"Did you smell horses? Did you hear them?"

"Yeah. What the hell is going on?"

"I don't know," admitted Duval. "But keep your eyes open."

Moreau nodded and moved away.

"Hey, where we going, anyway?" someone asked.

"Another merde village."

"This one's special," said Charette, a small, weasly man. "I heard about it back at headquarters."

"Why's that?"

"They had an interrogation team out there, and things got rough. They hurt some villagers, had to shoot a couple. There was some weird old guy there, a sorcerer they said, who put a curse on them all. They spread it around as a big joke, but the last guy from that team just died."

"Tell it to the Legion, Charette. They eat that crap with a short spoon."

"I'm telling you, it's true. Remember that guy from Lyon, stepped on the mine two weeks ago? He was one. And the one who just died from snakebite? He was the last. Eight in the patrol. All dead."

"Yeah, I heard something about that, too."

"You'll burn in hell for telling lies. You really believe that stuff?"

"I'm just telling you what I heard."

"Hey, Duval, what about this witchcraft stuff?"

"Well, tribes like this have their own beliefs. The Montagnards, for example..."

60

"Sacre, sorry I asked, professor." The laughter rang out in the hot air.

"Cut the chatter." The sergeant had appeared out of nowhere and stood glaring at them. "If you got that much energy, I guess you can march. Get up."

The sergeant kicked savagely at a few booted feet that were slow to move. When Duval looked at him, he was startled to see the sergeant wearing a conical metal cap with a strip of metal that covered his nose. Duval had seen pictures of the Bayeaux Tapestry, and recognized it as a Medieval Norman helmet.

"What the hell are you staring at?" the sergeant snarled.

"I...nothing, sergeant." The odd helmet was suddenly gone, replaced with the regulation one they all wore.

"Do you have a problem, Duval?" the sergeant leaned in, very close. His eyes glittered, and Duval felt real fear.

"Nothing, sergeant, nothing at all. It's just the heat."

"You give me a hard time, you'll have more than heat to worry about. Alright, let's go!" He shouted to the others, and moved out to take his advance post. The rest of the men shuffled slowly into line. Duval looked around for his arrows, and frowned at not seeing them.

Arrows? Why had he thought of that? For just a moment, he had been sure he carried a quiver as part of his standard issue. He wondered what kind of hallucination could be shared, and he wondered if their food or water had been drugged somehow. He wanted to tell someone, tell them Moreau was seeing things too, but they were moving out. He had no choice but to join them.

And so they walked, through the jungle, the insects, and the stifling heat. Duval's legs and feet screamed at him to stop, but he pressed on. He felt the blisters pop inside his boots, and his skin rubbed raw in pain. His whole body was sweating, making him itch all over. An insect bit him hard, and he slapped at it. His pack felt like lead, and he thought that this must be a lot like Hell. A vine seemed to grab at him, and he pushed it away with his bayonet. They walked on through the heat and the eerie silence.

Duval forced himself to think about what he had seen. Memories seemed to float just outside his consciousness, events of things before his time. He saw fire, and people dying. He had the sense that something was going to happen, that there was death up ahead. He looked up, and now everyone was wearing the strange clothing and helmets.

"Lieutenant," he called out. The officer stopped, and so did everyone else. Duval jogged forward.

"What is it?"

"There's trouble up ahead, something wrong. I don't know what it is, but it's in that village we're going to. We can't go there."

"We have to go there, we have our orders. If there's trouble, we have our rifles and they have farm tools. Get back in line."

"What the hell is the problem here?" the sergeant barked.

"Corporal Duval seems to be having visions. He says there's trouble," the lieutenant sighed.

"There's trouble all right." The sergeant took two steps and struck Duval down with a blow to the head.

"Anyone else seeing things?" The sergeant looked from face to face. No one spoke or looked up as they scuffed the earth at their feet.

"Tell them," Duval pleaded, through the pain. "Tell them what you see. Moreau, say something."

The sergeant smiled and walked over to Moreau, who didn't meet his gaze. He put his face very close and spoke quietly. "Did you see anything, Private Moreau?"

There was an inaudible mumble.

"I can't hear you, Private."

"No, sergeant."

"No what?"

"No, I didn't see anything."

The sergeant glared a moment longer and shook his head in disgust. He walked back to the head of the line.

"I don't think that was entirely necessary, sergeant," the lieutenant said softly. The sergeant stared at him until the smaller man dropped his eyes, and without another word the sergeant stalked off into the brush.

"What are you trying to do? Get me in trouble?" Moreau whispered to Duval as he helped him up.

"We've got to tell them," Duval said weakly. "We can't go into that village. Something bad is going to happen."

"Something bad will happen if you don't get moving."

"Look at me," Duval pointed down at his clothes, almost hysterical. "I'm wearing chain mail!"

"Snap out of it!" Moreau shook him. "You're a soldier and we've got a job to do."

"But there's going to be killing!"

"It's a war. There's always killing." Moreau turned and started walking.

Defeated and drained, Duval followed, hearing the clatter of swords and the clank of ammo clips.

They broke from the jungle, coming out on top of a ridge, with the village below. They saw the sergeant a short distance ahead, waving them on. They moved down the hill and crossed a crude footbridge over a stream. The village was like a hundred others the soldiers had seen, a seemingly random collection of flimsy shacks, with animals everywhere. The villagers saw them coming and stood watching, silent and sullen. Soldiers always meant trouble.

The sergeant kicked at a pig that had come too close, and it ran away squealing. A man who must have been the village headman talked rapidly to the sergeant, who pointedly ignored him. The headman then turned to the lieutenant, who waved Duval forward. Duval began the routine questioning, asking the headman if anyone in the village had seen any enemy. The man vehemently denied the presence of any enemy, and claimed the undying loyalty of everyone in the village. Duval asked him if they had any weapons or food stashed for the enemy. The man almost wept his denial.

Duval translated for the lieutenant, who looked bored. They had all been through this before.

"He says they have nothing, sir, that they are simple villagers. They have not seen the enemy, and would not help them if they had. They have no weapons or extra food."

"Naturally," the lieutenant said.

"Alright, let's begin," said the sergeant.

They split up into teams and began searching the huts. Villagers who moved to block any entrances were pushed aside. Duval continued to question the headman, who stridently denied any enemy contact.

It was then that Duval noticed the other man, small and very old, watching them intently. He was oddly dressed in animal skins, and held a staff with a tiny skull on top. Duval felt a shock of recognition, but could not say where he had seen the man before.

As the men of the patrol stabbed their swords into bags of rice and overturned things while checking the floors and walls, Duval knew the terrible thing was about to break. The men came back out of the huts, fowl cackling around their feet.

The sergeant moved toward one of the other huts, and the headman ran over and grabbed his arm, trying to stop him. The sergeant snarled and struck the man, brushing him aside like a curtain.

Only the drawn swords and bows held back the excited villagers, who seemed ready to break into a riot. Duval blinked. The sergeant emerged from the hut with a triumphant grin, towing a young woman by the wrist. She was barely more than a girl, and Duval knew her father had tried to hide her for fear of what the soldiers would do, what they always did. The sergeant bent down by a cooking fire and grabbed the unlit end of a burning stick with his free hand. He tossed the stick against the dry thatch of the hut, which crackled and spread the fire. The girl screamed, and the sergeant slapped her, then dragged her into one of the other huts.

Several of the villagers broke away to fight the blaze, and the men let them go. Duval shouted to them, and realized he had spoken to them not in Vietnamese nor French, but a foreign language he couldn't even name. He saw another hut take fire, shimmer, and change shape. The old man lifted his staff and began to chant.

A scream broke through the babble. The sergeant lurched from the doorway of the hut, eyes and mouth wide. He staggered a moment before falling face down in the dirt, the handle of a knife protruding from his neck. Soldiers and villagers stood unmoving for a moment. The girl came to the door of the hut, fierce hatred blazing in her eyes. She held her torn blouse together and spat on the body of the sergeant.

Over the crackle of the fire, Duval heard the twang of a bowstring. The girl fell back against the doorway, an arrow in her middle. She slid down the frame and crumpled in a heap. There were more shouts through the smoke from the blazing huts. Duval saw the old man making peculiar motions. The running figures were all dressed differently, and there was confusion everywhere.

Someone thrust a torch into a soldier's face. The screaming man staggered backward, and was pushed into one of the burning huts before it collapsed on him. Another villager ran up behind a soldier and struck him down with an axe. The soldier fell and didn't move.

Duval saw Moreau trip over a running pig and sprawl flat on his back. Before Moreau could get up, a villager darted in and drove a spear into his groin. The lieutenant was clubbed to the ground and stabbed. Duval tried to fire his rifle, and saw he was holding a short sword instead. The world shimmered and roared, and Duval ran from the carnage.

He made it through the smoke to the footbridge. Someone leaped at him, brandishing a knife. Duval yelled as he swung his blade, and felt it connect. The blade embedded itself, and Duval was pulled off balance as his opponent crumpled. On his hands and knees, Duval looked into the face of a young boy. The child's eyes were open and surprised, and Duval wept. The boy's features flickered and changed, showing several different nationalities.

The memories came rushing in, a torrential river of time. This was not the first episode, Duval now understood. That had been on the first Crusade, when Duval, a squire, had burned the village along with the men-at-arms. They had found no Saracens, but had destroyed the village anyway. The villagers attacked them with the tools at hand, and the village sorcerer had cursed them.

The slaughter had continued throughout the centuries, in many lands, and the bloody memory of it all flooded through Duval's mind. They had done the same thing with the armies of the Duc D'Orleans, with Louis the Sun King, with Napoleon's ravaging horde. Death and blood in endless cycles of savage pain. War was death and destruction, and they had delivered many into its embrace.

Duval understood that he was always the one to escape, to tell of what had happened, which always brought more death. Nothing was ever learned, and so the cycle was repeated. It had to stop. Duval looked at the dying boy, his life spilling away, along with all promise, all hope. Duval picked up the boy, so very light. He walked back toward the burning village. The enraged villagers took the boy from him.

Overwhelmed by the image of endless centuries of misery, Duval made no move to resist when they bound him. They pierced and rended his flesh, and his screams rang out amidst the smoke. His last view was of the shaman, looking at him and nodding. Duval wanted so much to die, not just for this time, but for always.

MOOSE TRACKS

"Killing a moose is a lot like going shopping," said Lou, who drove with only one hand on the wheel. With the other, he gestured toward the back, where two men sat on both sides of a large cooler. "Hand me another PBR, there, Harold ole chum."

"How so?" said Bud, who sat in the passenger seat of the big 4-by-4.

"Weh-ell," Lou said, drawing the word out to about three and a half syllables. He took the beer handed to him, wiped the can on his pant-leg to rid it of some clinging watery ice, set the can on his knee, and popped the top with an expert finger. He drank deeply, then went on.

"Mostly because you just have to get out to where they are, usually some swampy bog, and then just go pick it up. It's so damned easy to track them. They leave tracks the size of dinner plates, so big a kid could follow 'em."

"And when you find one, they don't usually startle off," said Chuck, from the back seat.

Lou shot a long look over his shoulder, like he didn't like being interrupted. Chuck lowered his head and kept quiet. Lou turned his gaze back to the dirt road, and went on.

"You can take your time picking your shot. Like picking the right fruit at the market. Pow, they fall over. Fill your basket. Hell, you could walk up to some of them and use your rifle as a club. They got no fear."

"They're so big," said Bud.

"Yeah, but we're the dominant species," replied Lou, and glanced back. The two men in the rear chuckled approvingly. "Sure they're big, like a steam locomotive. If they charge you, get the hell out of the way, for sure. Hell, you hit one with a car, the damn thing walks away, and you're totaled. But while we got our rifles, they're just meals on the hoof."

"Doesn't sound like a lot of challenge," said Bud.

"Aw, hell, kid, it's still hunting. You still gotta get a clean shot. If you just wound the thing, it'll take off and you'll have to track it through miles of swamp. Might miss out on a load of moose meat."

"What's the plural of moose?" said Harold from the back.

"Shitload of moose," said Lou, glancing into the rearview mirror for a reaction. The two backseaters cracked up like it was the first time they'd heard this joke.

Lou smiled to himself and pressed the button to roll down the window. He crumpled the now-empty can in his fist and tossed it out the window, then pressed the button again to roll the window back up. He snapped his fingers and held out his hand, and Harold retrieved another Pabst from the cooler and dutifully handed it over.

"You shouldn't be littering," said Bud, with a frown on his face. There was a silence in the vehicle.

"Hell, kid, you still got a lot to learn yet," said Lou. "You sound like some damned tree-hugger. Look around. This is the friggin' Allagash. Thousands of square miles of nothing. You think one little beer can is gonna make a difference?"

Bud reddened. "And there's a fine."

Lou laughed. "Like there's a lot of litter patrol cops out here?" The other two men joined in the laughter. "And besides, if we did get stopped, it'd be better not to have empty beer cans all over. Right?"

"I guess so."

"You guess right. I suppose next you'll tell me I shouldn't be drinking and driving."

Bud said nothing, looking out the window.

"Hell, boy, I been driving these roads and drinking beer since I was sixteen. What's that, thirty-two years? If nothing's happened in that long, it ain't likely to now. So don't get your panties in a twist. Hell, there ain't nothing out here to hit anyway."

"Logging truck," said Harold.

Lou gave a quick glare into the rearview, then grinned.

"Hell, we meet a logging truck, we're all dead anyway. Sonsabitches take the whole damn road, come barrel-assin' right down the middle."

Everyone was quiet at that.

"Jesus, what a bunch of pussies," said Lou, shaking his head. "You want to worry, you ought to think about real dangers out here."

"Like what?"

"Like stepping where you shouldn't and sinking down so fast you don't get found. Some of that bog ground is so swampy, it's like quicksand. Bloop, down you go, before you get a chance to think about it."

"For real?" said Bud.

"What, think I'm pulling your leg?" said Lou. "And other hunters. You get some idiots out here full of Jack Daniels, will shoot at any sound. So there might be a stray bullet come flyin' by."

"Now I know you're kidding," said Bud.

"Think so, huh?" Lou half-turned. "Harold, what year was that?"

"Ninety seven," replied Harold.

"Ninety seven," said Lou. "Chuck wasn't with us then, he was having his balls cut."

"What?" Bud said, startled.

"Vasectomy," Lou grinned. "Got chopped, and during hunting season, no less."

"You know I didn't have a choice on that, Lou," Chuck didn't sound happy.

"Yeah, not if you wanted to get it ever again. Anyway, it was Harold and I, and Buster Gilmore and Fatty Keaton. We were out at site eight."

"Think it was nine, Lou," Harold said.

Lou gave another look into the mirror. "It was eight."

"But you had that blue Chevy pickup. We didn't go out to eight that year."

"Whatever," Lou snapped. He buttoned down the window and flipped out his can. The window went back up and he held out his hand for another. "Make yourself useful."

The beer was passed, wiped, and opened in a smooth routine born of long practice.

"Anyway," Lou continued, after he had taken a swallow. "There we were, on the track of a big sumbitch, a bull. Then I hear a whack in the tree right next to me, not more 'n two feet away. You could tell it was a bullet. Harold 'bout like to shit his pants."

"Aw, come on, Lou," Harold chuckled, a pleading, uncomfortable sound.

"We dug that puppy out of the wood, looked like a thirty-ought-six, best we could tell. Two more steps, and I'd have got it right in the temple. I was some damned mad, I can tell you that. Looked for that peckerwood all afternoon, never found him."

"Jesus," said Bud.

"So I'm just saying, while all this may look easy, there's all kinda things to watch out for. Least of your worries is the moose. They're so damn stupid, even Chuck here is smarter. But take Harold now. He's so jittery on the trigger. He might shoot you by accident, instead of the moose."

"Looks like the fog's closing in," said Harold.

"Just a morning mist. It'll burn off," said Lou.

"Fog in a bog," said Chuck. Lou looked up at the mirror and shook his head.

"Tell us again why you're wearing camo," said Lou, grinning. "Afraid the moose are gonna see you and run?"

"It's my hunting gear," said Chuck.

"So what? You gonna disappear into the trees like a ninja? How the hell we gonna see you? Oh, yeah, the orange vest. Really goes with the camo." Lou laughed loudly, but seemed to be the only one doing it.

The four men were spread out in a line. Lou held up his hand, and they all stopped.

"See that?" Lou pointed at the ground. Bud peered down at some large dents in the soil. "There's your first moose tracks, kid."

"Man, they are big," Bud said. He squatted, noting some moisture in the bottom of the dents. "And they look pretty fresh."

"Jeez," said Lou. "First trip, and the kid's Daniel Boone already. Alright, Daniel. Let's go find us a moose to kill."

They moved off again, Bud excited now. When they came to the edge of a small, fetid pond, Lou tucked his rifle under his arm and passed binoculars to Bud.

"See if he's out there." Lou took a flask out of his hunting vest, uncapped it, and took a long swallow.

"Come on, Bullwinkle," said Harold.

"Thought I saw a flying squirrel," Chuck added. When Lou looked at him, he shrugged. "Just kidding. Hey, did you guys hear something?"

"Just your gums flapping," Lou said.

Bud set his rifle against a tree and looked through the binoculars, scanning the edge of the pond.

"I see one!" he said, his voice rising in excitement. "Over there." He passed the binoculars back to Lou, who had already tucked the flask back in place. Lou took a one-handed look and nodded.

"That's a real-life moose, alright," said Lou. "A cow. That's a female moose to you, Chuck. I guess she'll do. So let's get closer."

Twenty minutes later, they stopped in a small copse of spruce. The had a clear line of sight to the feeding moose, about eighty yards away.

"First one's mine," said Lou. He took up his rifle and wrapped the sling around his arm, steadying it further against the trunk of one of the spruces. The other men stepped back, giving him room.

"Wait," said Chuck. "I know I heard something behind us."

"Shut up," said Lou. "I'm taking the shot."

"Listen," said Chuck. There was a loud crackling close by, as if something was snapping through the brush.

"Keep your damn mouth shut," hissed Lou. "Or I'll shut it for you."

Bud was watching the feeding moose, and so was taken by surprise. From behind them, something huge smashed into and through the men, scattering them like wisps of straw. Bud was knocked to the ground, and a great weight descended on his leg. He heard the snap, and screamed. His head jerked up, and he saw a wall of brownish-black fur in motion.

Bud looked over at Lou, who also lay on the ground and was trying to raise the rifle. But a spindly brown leg knocked into the weapon, and a loud crack split the air.

Bud gasped, holding his leg. He saw the antlers now, high up off the ground, and knew they'd been charged by a bull moose, probably the mate of the one feeding nearby. He watched as the moose raised a hoof and brought it down on Lou. Horrified, he saw a gargantuan hoof cover Lou's head and press down. He heard yelling from either Harold or Chuck, he didn't know which.

Having just seen Lou get trampled, Bud felt a surge of adrenaline and got up on his one good knee. He used the tree to struggle to a standing position.

The bull was turned away from him. Bud grabbed a branch of the spruce and pulled himself up. A bolt of pain ripped through his leg, but he got a foothold on a low branch with the other leg and boosted himself up. He risked a look.

Harold was on his knees, arms wrapped around his middle. His face was ashen. Bud saw blood and realized that Lou's shot had struck Harold by accident. Bud clutched at a higher branch and pulled up, getting one rung higher before glancing back.

Chuck was chest-high in a patch of muck, unable to escape. As Bud watched, the moose reached out with a front hoof and deliberately pushed down on Chuck's head. Chuck sank further into the mire, and screamed once before the black goop closed over his face. Only his arms could be seen now.

Terror gave Bud strength, and helped him set aside the pain as he moved up from branch to branch, ignoring the slapping of spruce limbs. He did not stop until he reached up and realized he could not go any further. He looked down and saw he was a good twenty feet from the ground.

The bull was facing him now, but Bud was out of reach. Bud gasped with his exertions, and wondered if the bull would ram the tree to try to knock him down.

Bud looked behind the moose. Harold lay on the ground, not moving, one arm now splayed out. Lou's head was unrecognizable as such. No trace of Chuck could be seen in the black patch. Bud sobbed, as the moose watched him with an unruffled calm.

Bud clung to the tree, praying for deliverance. He felt horrified at the thought of being crushed to death under the cruel hoofs of the beast below. He closed his eyes and gripped the trunk tightly.

When he finally opened his eyes, he saw that the bull had joined up with the female they had almost shot. The two moose gave him a last look and then turned and walked away. Bud was so relieved, he almost fell from the tree.

No one believed him, of course. He barely escaped being prosecuted, and was considered to have lost his reason out in the Allagash. It was not unheard of, after all. But people knew what was true, and what wasn't. If they couldn't explain something, it wasn't true. After all, we're the dominant species. All Bud knew was, he'd never follow moose tracks again.

BODY ENGLISH

"Ready?" asked Liz.

Tom Shea had been lost in thought, and the question from his wife startled him.

"Sure," he lied. He doubted if anyone was ever really ready for a funeral like this. Not when the deceased was your friend's wife, and you were to blame for her death.

Tom closed the book he hadn't really been reading. He stumbled out from the den, got his keys, and went out to the car. Liz got in, and they drove to Henry's place in silence.

Henry sat on the couch in his living room, staring at nothing.

"Henry?" Liz said, her voice soft.

"Yes?" He looked up, his eyes swollen and red.

"It's time to go," she said.

"Oh," was all he said. He rose from the couch as if going to his own execution. When he left, Tom noticed Henry hadn't even locked the door.

They rode in silence to the cemetery. Tom was glad to be driving, so he wouldn't need an excuse not to look at Henry. They parked and walked over to the solemn-looking minister.

The mourners, many of them colleagues of Tom and Henry, trickled in, offering their condolences. When they spoke to Tom, he made small talk, and agreed what a terrible tragedy it was.

When Henry had remarried at 58, it put the small college community into shock. His new, young wife Terry drank too much, flirted too much, and wore clothes considered too revealing.

Then Tom and Liz began to have problems. Liz wanted Tom to take a better paying position at another college. Tom felt that would be deserting Henry, who had pulled strings to get Tom his current position.

One night they had got into a bad argument. Liz accused Tom of encouraging Terry, and he had been nasty in turn. She had stormed off, leaving him alone. He mooned about the place, feeling sorry for himself, and started drinking.

Two hours later, Tom's doorbell rang. It was Terry, and she had followed him in. When she found out Liz was gone, she had smiled and poured herself a drink. Tom had another as well. They each had several more. Before long, they were necking on the couch. Then things went further.

The next morning, Tom was hung over and ashamed. When Liz returned, she took his abashed behavior for contrition.

One rainy afternoon when Liz was out grocery shopping, Terry showed up again, drunk and wet from the rain. Tom only let her in when she threatened to scream on his doorstep.

She'd marched over to the liquor cabinet and poured herself a drink. She'd said nothing. Tom could still vividly remember what had happened.

"Do you think it's a good idea to be drinking this early?"

"I think it's a great idea," she snarled.

"Terrific. What are you doing here?"

"I just came over for a little company. I wanted to see my old friend Tommy. I thought maybe he could help me out of these wet clothes."

"What happened before was an accident, a mistake. It never should have happened, and it's not going to happen again."

"Is that so?" She took a large swallow of scotch. "Why don't you have a drink? You're much more fun when you drink."

"You're not. You better leave."

"I'll go when I'm damned good and ready," she slammed her drink on the bar. "Oh, look at what you've done. You made me spill my drink, you naughty boy. I better make another one."

"Take the whole bottle. Enjoy it. But go."

"What's the matter? Don't feel like it today? Don't feel like cheating with your friend's wife to pay back the mousey little shrew?"

"Shut up, just shut up!"

"Come on, I can keep a secret. Is Tommy-boy afraid of his wife? Afraid little Lizzie will cry?"

"Get out of here," Tom said, advancing on her.

"Or what?" she snapped. "You going to beat me up? Or tell Henry? Fat chance. You know how jealous he gets. We wouldn't want poor Tommy to lose his job now, would we?" Terry's smile was pure malice.

"Can't we forget this ever happened?"

"Right. Tommy's had his fun, and now he feels all sorry. What I want doesn't matter, you're all through with me. Well maybe I'm not through with you."

"Don't do anything stupid."

"I already have!" she screamed. "I come to this rathole town and find there's no real men. I'm on a short leash with a husband who goes crazy every time a man tries to talk to me. I thought you might be good for some laughs, but you turn out to be a bastard just like the rest of them. I hate you! I hate you all!"

Terry hurled her drink against the wall, where it exploded in a shower of glass. She stormed out, slamming the door behind her. Tom shook as he cleaned up the mess.

Soon after, the police had pulled Terry's body from the twisted wreck of her car. Tom was horrified when he realized how relieved he was.

When the service ended, Henry stayed behind after everyone else had left. Tom and Liz waited by the car, letting him grieve and say goodbye in private.

"He's taking it hard," she said.

"Yeah," said Tom. "But then, so would I if anything happened to you."

Liz looked up and half-smiled. She hugged him, and they clung to each other. Tom felt a surge of hope that things might actually work out. He had come so close to losing it all.

Henry came back with the look of a man given in to total despair. On the way back he just stared out the window.

"Henry?" Liz said. "Do you want to stay with us? We could fix up the extra room, and you wouldn't have to be alone."

"No, thank you. I... I need to be by myself for awhile."

"Are you sure? You might be better off with us, just for a day or two."

"No, that's alright, I'll be fine."

"You know, if there's anything you need..."

"I know. Thank you. You've both been so good to me, I don't know what I would have done without you."

Tom gripped the steering wheel, fighting to hold back guilty tears. Henry went into his house, moving slowly.

Tom took Henry's classes as well as his own that week, trying to bury himself in work. He came home on Friday tired, but beginning to forgive himself.

"Hi there," Liz greeted him. "Hope you didn't have any big plans for tomorrow."

"Why, what's up?"

"Henry asked us to come over and go through Terry's things. He couldn't bear to do it. He'll even cook supper for us, something special. Says he needs the company."

All the guilt Tom had tried to forget came flooding back. He got no sleep that night.

The next day in Henry's house, Tom was tormented by every piece of Terry's clothing, everything that had once belonged to her. When they got to the bedroom, Tom almost broke down. While packing clothes into a box for Goodwill, he spied a red leather-bound diary, and panicked. What if Terry had written about that night? He would lose Liz, his job, everything.

"Hey, hon?" He tried to keep his voice casual, but to him it sounded strained and artificial. "We're almost done in here. Why don't I finish up, and you start on the bathroom."

"Good idea," Liz agreed. As soon as she left, Tom snatched at the book. He scanned the pages, looking for any damning passages. He didn't hear Liz come back in.

"Have you seen the..." she stopped as he snapped the book shut, flushing a guilty crimson.

"What is that?" she said, stepping closer. "A diary?"

He nodded, the sound of his heart pounding in his ears. Liz looked at him, hr lips forming a thin line.

"Give it to me." She held out her hand. He could think of no way to refuse, and handed over his destruction. Then he could not believe his luck when she dropped the diary in the bag for trash.

"I don't think anyone needs to read this, especially now. You should be ashamed of yourself." She took the bag and left the room. Tom's knees wobbled, and he almost cried with relief as he leaned on the dresser for support.

It took all afternoon to remove everything. When they finished, Henry seemed in good spirits.

"I really can't thank you two enough," he said. "You've done so much." Henry looked straight at Tom when he spoke. "I've already made dinner, so you might as well stay and relax. I know you've been working hard."

"Well…" said Liz.

"Please don't go. Stay and have some wine. I… I could use the company."

"Of course we'll stay," said Liz, with a glance at Tom. "Do you need any help in the kitchen?"

"No, no, I'm all done. Just have a seat."

Henry returned with three crystal wine glasses filled with a ruby liquid.

"A toast," Henry said dramatically. "To the immortal Bard. Like another, I have loved not wisely, but too well."

Tom and Liz felt uncomfortable, but drank because Henry did. There was an odd, unpleasant flavor to the wine, which surprised Tom, because Henry's taste was usually so good.

"What is this, anyway?" he asked.

"A Merlot. It'll go well with the lamb."

"I'm surprised at you," said Tom. "Not letting a good red breathe first."

Henry looked at him. "Oh, I let it breathe, all right. Wanted to make sure it was just right for my very special friends. It is all right isn't it?"

"Sure," Tom lied. Liz smiled and made polite chatter, so Tom sat back and sipped some more, accepting the bitter taste as part of his punishment. He refused to hurt Henry's feelings tonight.

After dinner, Henry pleaded with them to sit for awhile and talk before going home. He made a fire in the fireplace, and as it grew dark outside, they sat and watched it crackle, talking only of safe subjects. Tom felt his head getting fuzzy, and wondered how he could get drunk on so little wine. He felt sleepy, and saw Liz curled up in a corner of the couch.

It took effort for Tom to turn back to Henry. No one had spoken for awhile. He tried to move, but a fog had settled in his brain, and it was just too hard to rise. Henry swam into view, staring at him.

"How are you feeling?" Henry's voice was muffled, as if he were talking in a tunnel.

"Sleepy," slurred Tom. "Liz too."

"Must be the wine," Henry snickered.

Tom tried to shake his head to clear the cobwebs, but found he couldn't. Henry's face got more blurry.

"Should go."

"Go?" Henry echoed. "Oh, no, you're going to stay. My little party's just starting."

He reached out and slapped Tom hard. Tom was shocked, and the blow cleared his head somewhat. He still couldn't move, despite the pain.

"You bastard!" Henry hissed, his face close. "You and my wife. I get you this job, give you my friendship, and you sneak behind my back. She was all I had! How happy you must have been when she hit that tree. You thought you were free and clear, didn't you? Did you see her diary today? Did you read it?

"All because of you. The drinking, the accident. Well, you killed her, and I've got another surprise for you."

Henry laughed, and the only movement from Tom was a flicker of his eyes.

"You were so concerned for me, and all the while I was preparing my surprise. I thought you were catching on when you mentioned letting the wine breathe. Bitter, wasn't it? But everything worked well. You can feel absolutely everything I do, but you can't lift a finger. We have quite a time ahead of us."

Henry kept laughing as a tiny tear squeezed out of Tom's eye and rolled down the immobile face. Henry brought out the knife and gently caressed Tom's cheek.

Dale T. Phillips

THE SILVER WEB

By Dale Phillips and Tom Chenelle

The storm blew up suddenly, as if out of nowhere, and crashed down around the boy, cracking thunder exploding like doom itself. Twelve-year-old Barry Braden cowered under the onslaught, as a torrent of rain sliced down with a seeming malevolence. Only a minute before, the sky had but few clouds in the last waning glow of sunset. Now all was black, except when the garish lightning illumined everything with a fearsome, unworldly glow. The wind moaned like a wild thing in pain, whipping across the top of the reservoir, roiling the surface of the water within the barriered embankment.

Another flash, another deafening barrage of thunder, and a nearby oak tree burst asunder, as if made of glass. What remained was aflame, and all the boy could do was stare.

Barry looked down at the strip of soft silver around his wrist, the shard he had pried loose from the ground. In the late afternoon sun he had spotted the gleam from the earth beneath his feet, and stopped to investigate. Finding it to be a vein of metal, with a length not buried by the surrounding rocks, he had wrenched at a section until it came loose, the piece he now held. The torn ends of the greater part oozed as if wounded. As the part came free, the storm had descended, and the fear struck him that he had brought the deluge.

Another monstrous crack roused him, and he slid down the muddy embankment and ran for his life. Lashed on by the gale, he soon reached his physical limit. Barry felt weaker somehow, as if something were tapping into his life force and draining away his energy. Falling in the mud, the boy sobbed in terror.

With another phosphorescent flash, the area was lit up, and Barry thought he saw a shelter. He scrambled up and ran in the direction of his vision, praying for relief. His heart leapt when he confirmed the reality of a small hut, abandoned and dark, but still affording some protection from the elements.

The old door sported a rusty padlock. Barry cracked the flimsy wood with several kicks, until the door popped loose. Once inside, Barry crawled to a corner, and lay shivering in a drenched misery. He covered his ears and closed his eyes against the brutal pounding outside, and lay curled up and whimpering.

"Hell of a storm," Tom Leffingham said, shaking the raindrops from his slicker before hanging it on the row of hooks. His shirt was wet, too, but he had a spare in his locker. He unhooked his Town Sheriff badge and put it in his pants pocket. He wanted to get dry and get a cup of coffee. It looked to be a long night.

Gale, the dispatcher looked up.

"Sure is. Power's out in over half the town."

"Great. It'll be crazy tonight."

"Already is. Bob's out on the Powerline Road, Andy's on Eastlake Drive, and Marco's downtown. Oh, and you got a call from Theresa Braden. Her son Barry was out when the storm hit. He was riding his bike down by the reservoir. She's worried about him."

Tom sighed. "He may just be trying to stay dry somewhere, but I better have a look. Kid shouldn't be out in this. No one should."

Tom turned back to his wet slicker. There was no point in changing to a dry shirt now. He pulled the raincoat from the hook and went back out to do his job.

Tom's cruiser made it, but not by much. Twice he had to stop for branches that had fallen and blocked the road. He was able to move them off to the ditch at the side and continue on. The road around the reservoir was a dirt track, and the torrential rain had quickly turned it soft and treacherous for vehicular traffic. Tom stopped the car when his headlights picked out a bike, laid on its side at the base of the short slope of the reservoir.

Tom got out with his powerful flashlight, and squatted to inspect the bike. He put it in the trunk of his cruiser and continued on foot, sweeping the area in broad arcs with the beam. He knew there was a small pumphouse hut a short distance away, and headed in that direction. The rain made tracking the boy impossible, but Tom bet on the shack as the most likely spot for Barry to be.

Tom reached the place a short time later, and saw the busted door. He stepped inside and flashed the light around the interior. There was the boy, huddled in the corner. Tom knelt by his side. The boy was unconscious, his body shivering with hypothermia. Tom chided himself for not bringing a blanket, but he doubted it would have stayed dry anyway. He tucked the flashlight away and picked the boy up. As best he could, he headed back to the cruiser.

Half an hour later, Tom looked up as Doctor Perkins came out to the visitor's lounge. Theresa Braden beat him to the question.

"He's alright, isn't he?"

"As best we can tell," said the doctor soothingly. "He's asleep now, we got his temperature regulated. We'll know more in the morning. You should go home and get some rest."

"I'll give you a ride," offered Tom, but the woman shook her head.

"I'm not going anywhere until I know for sure he's okay."

Tom looked at the doctor, who shrugged. Tom sighed and rose to go.

"I'll check back in the morning," he said.

Tom was busy all night on calls for one thing or another, and was exhausted by ten the next morning. He wanted to sleep, but stopped by the hospital to check on Barry Braden.

Day had brought no relief from the weather, the storm still in full fury, the daytime sky unnaturally dark. And if Tom thought he would find a tired but happy Theresa Braden, he was shocked to find her frantic and horrified. She had been sitting with another woman, but jumped to her feet when Tom arrived.

"What is it?" Tom said. "What's wrong?"

"Barry," Theresa croaked, her voice harsh with strain. "Something's wrong. He wasn't outside for that long was he? That wouldn't matter, would it?"

"Of course not," Tom said. "Let me talk to the doctor."

It was a different doctor on duty this morning, and he frowned at Tom's question.

"I don't know what to tell you," he said, looking embarrassed. "The boy is running a high fever, and we can't seem to bring it down. He's had convulsions from time to time, and is in some sort of delirium, babbling strangely. We've run tests, but..."

"I want to see him."

"All right. We had to ask his mother to leave the room, she was getting frantic."

They walked down the hall, and the doctor opened the door to one of the rooms. A nurse looked at them as they entered. Tom gazed at the small form in the big bed.

"He seems okay now," he looked at the doctor.

"It comes and goes. Sometimes--" the doctor never finished, as a strange series of sounds came from the boy, loud and harsh. It seemed to be a language, but none that Tom had ever heard.

"What the hell is that?" Tom looked back at the doctor again.

"Beats me. Nothing I know of. Maybe it's Klingon."

Tom looked at the doctor closely. The doctor turned red.

"I'm serious. Hear those glottal stops? That's the closest thing to it. They have books where kids can learn it, even a summer camp. Maybe." The doctor shrugged.

"I'll check with his mother," Tom said. "But it sure sounds weird."

"He'll do it for a few minutes and stop. About every half hour or so."

Tom stepped closer. The boy's head rolled from side to side as he uttered the strange words. The boy's arm twitched as if touched with an electrical wire. Tom looked more closely at the arm, and saw a silver bracelet around the boys' wrist.

"What's that?" He asked, pointing to the bracelet.

"Don't know. He had it when he came in. There's some writing on it."

Tom knelt and put his face close to the piece. He saw a flowing script, but the symbols were in an unknown alphabet. He straightened up and shook his head.

"Too many strange things going on. I'll go have a talk with his mother."

Having got no helpful information from Theresa Braden about the boy's mutterings or the odd jewelry, Tom went home, peeled off his wet clothes, and quickly collapsed into bed.

Tom was awakened five hours later by the ring of the telephone. Groggy and cursing gently, he recognized Gale's voice.

"Tom?"

"Yeah."

"It's Barry Braden. He's... he's dead, Tom."

Tom sat up, suddenly awake. "What happened?"

"They don't know. They say he just got weaker until his heart stopped. Oh, Tom, he was only twelve."

Tom rubbed his face. "I know Gale, I'm sorry. His mother at the hospital?"

"She had to be sedated. She went a little crazy, not that you can blame her."

"Alright, I'm going to shower and come on in. I'll swing by the hospital." Tom heard something tapping on the side of his house, probably the tree branch he'd been meaning to take down. It always rapped on the house in a good wind.

"Don't tell me the storm's still going?"

"Hasn't let up for a minute."

"So what did he die of?" Tom looked at the medical examiner.

"Can't really say until we do an autopsy," the man replied. "The best I can give you without a closer examination is shock."

Tom looked at the boy's body, stretched out on the table, and suddenly felt old and weary, though he wasn't yet forty.

"Okay, please call me the moment you have anything."

"Will do. His stuff is over there, if you want to have a look."

Tom walked over to the sideboard, where a small carton held the boy's clothes and pocket items. Tom saw the silver bracelet and picked it up. He felt a mild tingle as he did, like there was a current going through the piece. Sort of like putting your tongue to a battery end. It was a bit slick, as if there was a light sheen of oil on the surface. He looked at the writing, the tiny symbols going the entire length of the piece. The ends were jagged, showing they had been torn, not machined. He flexed the metal strip, and it bent easily. The curve was irregular, showing that it had been more of a straighter piece, and likely the boy had bent it in an arc to place on his wrist. Tom was puzzled as to where the boy could have got the thing. There weren't any antique shops or jewelers in town, the closest one was over thirty miles away. Maybe a yard sale, or something he found in the trash, as his mother hadn't remembered his having the bracelet before. Tom hefted the piece, weighty for its size. Definitely a mystery beyond his police comprehension. This called for a more academic mind, and Tom knew just who to call.

"Professor Carlsen, thank you for taking the time to see me."

"Not at all, glad to be of help, if I can."

"Well, we're completely baffled, I can tell you. We have no idea what this thing is." Tom took the silver bracelet from a clear evidence bag and placed it on a sheet of paper on the professor's desk. The professor peered at it over his glasses, then took out a clean white handkerchief and picked the thing up. He turned it every which way, studying it. He brought out a magnifying glass, and studied the inscriptions. Tom waited patiently for him to finish. At last the professor put the bracelet back on the paper and sighed.

"I'm afraid I have no idea what this is."

Tom was crestfallen, hoping to have found some answers.

"Perhaps if I show you the CD," he said. "From the hospital room camera. They show the boy speaking in tongues. Maybe if you hear it--"

"Yes, of course I'll listen, but this is no language I know of," he said, tapping the bracelet. "It's not runic, or hieroglyphics, but it seems to be like those somehow, only more ancient. I couldn't begin to even pin it down as to part of the world."

Tom put the CD on the desk.

"I hate to ask for a rush job, but you understand..."

"Of course," said the professor. "I'll look at it right away. And I'll tell you what. If I still can't figure it out, I'll put it out on the Web. There's a couple of sites for odd things, maybe someone else will have an idea."

Tom stood up and shook hands.

"Thank you, Professor. It's pretty important. His mother is a complete wreck. She'd like some answers. We all would. There are some weird things going on, and I think this may have something to do with it, although I couldn't tell you why."

Most of the town resumed normal operations, despite the continuation of the storm. Tom got through the night, and had been sleeping for a few hours when his telephone woke him once again. He groggily reached for it, and thought he might disconnect it if this kept up.

"Tom here."

"Sheriff, it's Professor Carlsen. You said to call when I found something."

"What have you got?"

"It's not me, I couldn't figure the thing out, but I put a picture of the bracelet with the writing out on the Web, and included a sound file from what the boy had been saying. I just got off the phone with a Doctor Howard from Miskatonic University. He says he's figured out what the bracelet is, and is coming over to meet us at your office. He said he'd be there in about half an hour."

Tom squinted in thought. "But Miskatonic is sixty miles away."

"He says we're all in very great danger."

"From what?"

"He says he'll explain when he sees us. Oh. And one more thing. Can you get hold of a soldering kit?"

"Sure, I've got one downstairs. The pins are always coming loose from our badges. Why do you need it?"

"I don't know, but Doctor Howard said it was of the utmost importance."

"Alright, I'll see you there in about twenty minutes."

On the way to the office, Tom felt the tremors of the first earthquake. His car slewed to the side and almost went off the road. Shaken, he pulled over and radioed in.

"Gale what the hell was that? I'm coming in, and it felt like an earthquake."

A frightened Gale sounded small and far away.

"We got it here, too, The whole building shook. I have to go, Tom. The whole board is lighting up."

Tom figured it would be, with panicked calls from the townsfolk. First a never-ending storm, and now an earthquake? What the hell was going on?

The second major tremor hit as he walked in to the office. Tom stumbled and fell against a desk. People cried out in shock and fear. After ascertaining that no one was hurt, Tom checked with Gale and found there were fourteen 911 calls. They arranged for extra services from the nearby towns, and Tom looked up to see Professor Carlsen.

"I'll be right with you, as soon as we--"

Tom was cut off as the door slammed open and a wild-eyed, wild-haired man ran inside.

"Where is it? Where's the piece of the silver ring?"

"Who are you?" Tom realized that a lot was going on, and he didn't want yet another thing to deal with.

"Howard. Doctor Howard, from Miskatonic University. I must see the artifact."

"What are you talking about?"

Professor Carlsen held up the bracelet taken from Barry.

"Is this what you're referring to?"

Howard lunged and grabbed the bracelet from the professor's hand. He studied it intently, talking to himself, ignoring everyone in the room. In spite of everything going on, Tom watched him, the hairs on the back of his neck prickling.

"This is it. This is part of the Silver Ring. Where did you get it?"

The man looked around with a fierce glare, and everyone pulled back.

"I think I know about where it came from," Tom said. "What is it?"

"Then you must take me there. Right now."

"Tell me what it is."

"There's no time," snapped Howard. "It may already be too late. I'll explain on the way. You have a soldering kit?"

"It's in the car."

"We must find it. Now!"

In spite of the other emergency situations, Tom's instincts told him to do what the man said. He went out to the car, Howard and Professor Carlsen following. When they were outside, the ground spasmed again, throwing up chunks of the road high in the air.

"This is it," yelled Howard, above the howling of the wind. "He comes!"

"Who comes?" Tom asked.

"The Destroyer."

"What are you talking about?"

"No time. If he breaks through, we're all dead. Hurry."

Shaking his head in the driving rain, Tom opened the cruiser and started it up. The other two men got in. Tom put the cruiser in gear and headed for the reservoir, turning on his siren and speeding as fast as he could go.

"Now what's all this about?" Tom said.

Howard was in the passenger side. He held up the bracelet.

"This is part of The Silver Ring."

"What?"

"It was put in place to hold back the Destroyer. To keep him out."

"Who's the Destroyer?"

"An evil from ancient times, much longer ago than history records. At some time in the past, The Silver Ring was put in place to keep him from entering this world. You see the writing?"

"Yes, what is it?"

"It is from the Necronomicon."

"What's that?"

From the back, Professor Carlsen gasped.

"It actually exists?"

"It does," Howard said grimly. "Under guard at Miskatonic."

"Will one of you please tell me what is going on?" Tom tried to keep his attention on the road and the driving rain.

"Suffice to say," said Howard. "A madman created the book from visions, mostly hideous nightmares, of things from other worlds that threatened to come back to our plane of existence. This is one such. Long ago in the past, there were those who sought to hold back the darkness. They created a huge ring of silver, here in this town's location, beset with powerful magic verses, to hold back the one they call The Destroyer. His real name must never be spoken, but the in file Professor Carlsen put out on the Web, I heard it twice. For thousands of years he has remained in his world, but some fool has broken the Ring and loosed him."

"Wait a minute," said Tom. "You're saying some monster has been unleashed by Barry prying loose this little piece of metal?"

"It is no ordinary metal, but part of a larger piece. The integrity of the whole gives it the power."

"I don't believe it," said Tom. "This is crazy."

"Where do you think these earthquake tremors are coming from? He is trying to break through to this world. And this storm? Don't tell me you have storms like this that go on for days."

Tom was silent, and concentrated on his driving. His mind reeled. Here were two educated men telling him about monsters from another world, and he almost half believed it.

"So what do you want us to do?"

"We must find where the Ring was broken and repair it as best we can. It may not work, but we have no other choice. If we fail, our world is gone."

Tom looked in the rearview mirror to catch the eye of Professor Carlsen. He saw a frightened man, and it in turn frightened him. These men were nuts, plain and simple, but he'd better play along.

"There's the reservoir road," Tom said. He turned onto the dirt road, and manhandled the wheel as the cars tires hit the soft, mushy dirt. His cruiser was built for tough conditions, and they progressed where normal cars would have bogged down. Tom fought the slog around the reservoir, until they came close to the spot where he had found Barry's bike. He stopped the cruiser.

"It was around here," he said. "What should we look for?"

"This came out of the ground," said Howard. "That embankment. It goes around the reservoir?"

"Yes."

"Silver and water together have increased powers. The Ring is probably buried in that embankment. Look for a spot where the boy could have dug it from the earth."

"Looks pretty solid down here," said Tom. "Maybe on top?"

"Yes. And bring the soldering kit."

The three men got out of the car and scrambled as best they could up the wet embankment, getting rather muddy in the process. Tom reached the top first, and helped the others up with an extended hand. They reached the top and fanned out, scanning the ground closely.

"Here," said Professor Carlsen. "Look at this groove."

The others closed around and squatted to inspect the spot. Howard used his hands to wipe away the mud, and they saw the exposed ends of silver from under the rock. Howard stretched the silver band out straight, and set it between the ends, where it was a close fit.

"That's it. Solder this in, and hurry."

Tom flicked the switch to warm up the battery-powered soldering gun, the back of his mind wondering just how crazy these men were. But a sudden eruption of the ground around them knocked them all off balance, and they fell.

"He comes," screamed Howard, above the sound of the driving wind. "Hurry, for all that you hold dear."

Tom regained his balance and held the soldering gun next to the strip of silver. But it had not had time to warm up, and nothing happened. There was another shudder from the earth, and a giant crack of thunder. Tom was shocked to see the water draining from the reservoir, as if the plug had been pulled from a giant bathtub. The water poured down into the earth, and in three minutes the reservoir was completely emptied, millions of gallons gone into a sudden hole. Tom stared, watching the middle of the reservoir bed, a massive black trench in the earth. Something pushed up from the ground, raising a huge lump, pushing upward at a steady pace until it broke free.

Tom now saw something like a giant tree emerge from the black scar and push up, sprouting like Jack's beanstalk, rising rapidly. It had to be at least three hundred feet across. Tom tested the soldering gun in his hand, and it was finally hot enough. He bent to the task, soldering an end of the bracelet from Barry back to the vein of silver it had been torn from. He looked up, and the tree-like thing still rose, crashing up from the reservoir basin like a train tearing loose form the earth.

Doctor Howard smacked him on the back of his head.

"Finish it!" The man cried. "Don't look! It is madness!"

One end of the silver strip was soldered back into the vein from which it had come, and Tom applied himself to the other end. He heard a scream and looked up, as the ground shook with violent upheavals.

The thing that had sprouted from the earth now rose to several hundred feet. It was a grayish-green color, but looked alive. There was a large lump at the top, a swelling bubo. As he watched, a split appeared in the lump, and a section parted. A giant eye was revealed, and Tom heard a scream from behind him. He could not bear the sight or the thought of what was there, and he looked only at his task, soldering the one remaining end of the strip. As he did, he heard a gibbering, mad cadence behind him, some sort of incantation that Doctor Howard was reciting as fast as possible. From the corner of his eye, Tom saw Professor Carlsen grab his chest, as a grimace of pain crossed his face.

Tom whispered a prayer and applied the tip of the gun to the end of the metal strip, and watched as the strip fused with the piece in the ground. He heard more screaming, a pained sound that reached him over the tumult of the storm. The shaking ground trembled less, and suddenly the rain stopped slashing down at him. There was a hideous, unearthly shriek throughout the sky, a final flash of lightning, and Tom saw several hundred feet of writhing unexplainable something withdraw from the sky, back down into the black scar, disappearing into the earth.

There was a sudden quiet in the aftermath, and Tom looked down at his trembling hands, as tears coursed down his face.

Eventually, some people from the town came out to the spot by the drained reservoir, where, unbeknownst to them, Tom had saved them all. They found a raving lunatic, a dead man, and a white-haired former Town Sheriff, who, when they looked in his eyes, seemed to see other, far-off worlds they could not comprehend.

BLESS ME, FATHER

By Matt Phoenix

Father Tom took the seat across from his oldest friend and made space at the table by stacking half-eaten TV dinners and pushing aside empty liquor bottles.

"I killed her," Adam said, fidgeting with a dirty glass of whiskey and running his hand through his greasy hair. Food stains blotched the thick stubble around his mouth, and dark patches underlined his bloodshot eyes.

Father Tom knew that widowers often blamed themselves, but Adam's lack of personal hygiene alarmed him.

"I'm glad you asked me to come over. I'm worried about you. A lot of us are."

"Did you hear me? I said I killed Helen."

"It sounds like the first line of one of your old stories. It's called 'the hook', right?"

Father Tom heard a sound like a faraway backfire. Adam shot a look toward the cellar door, and then downed the contents of his glass.

"I killed her, Tommy. I'm not kidding."

Father Tom recoiled at the stench of body odor as Adam reached for a bottle of Jack Daniels.

"When was the last time you left the house? Or even this kitchen? Isn't that what you wore to the funeral? It's been more than a week."

Adam didn't respond, and Father Tom said, "The world is worse without Helen, and I'm sorry. But you can't let her death ruin your life. She wouldn't want that."

"She didn't want me getting her killed, either."

"Helen had a heart attack. It's an awful tragedy, but it's the truth. And as confusing as it may be, it's also part of God's plan."

Helen was only thirty-five and was in great shape, but the Thursday before last, her heart had simply stopped. Father Tom had also heard that if she had somehow managed to survive the coronary, the nasty fall down the cellar stairs probably would have killed her.

Father Tom put his hand on Adam's. "There's nothing you could've done."

"You're right. Once it started, there's nothing I could've done. I keep telling myself that."

"Right. See? Now you've got to pick up the pieces and get on with your life." Father Tom stood and gathered trash from the table. "Go take a shower and change your clothes. I'll clean up down here."

A loud bang from the cellar caused Father Tom to drop the stack of empty TV dinners. While he was down on his hands and knees using the edge of a tray to scrape apple cobbler off the floor, he felt a low rumbling beneath him.

"You should get your furnace checked. It sounds ready to die."

"It's not the furnace, it's the demon."

Father Tom looked up and found Adam staring out the window over the sink.

"Pardon?"

Adam turned to look at him. "The furnace is fine. The demon's making that noise."

Father Tom rocked back. The floor rumbled beneath him. He stood up, wiping finger trails of apple cobbler and cranberry sauce on his black linen pants. He opened his mouth to speak. Failed. Tried again. Nothing. Finally, he uttered, "What?"

"I summoned him," Adam said, plainly. "I was researching magical incantations for a story, and I stumbled across one of the documents found with the Gospel of Judas. I printed it out, then read it. I don't know how, it was no language I'd ever seen, but it was as easy to read as Dick and Jane."

Father Tom's face scrunched up in disbelief. "Come on. This is not H.P. Lovecraft. You can't just Google up the Necronomicon and summon a demon. Do you even hear yourself?"

"Helen thought I was nuts, too."

"This was going on before she died?"

Father Tom, incredulous, dropped into the chair, rested his forehead against his palms, elbows on his knees. Now he understood why Helen had kept trying to reach him.

"At the beginning, everything was fine. Great, actually. I wrote a dozen stories in the first four weeks after summoning him. I haven't written that much since before I got married. And every one sold. All these editors who'd been sending me form rejections for years were now begging for more. The demon was my muse and good luck charm all in one." Adam let his eyes drift like a child being scolded. "Then he demanded payment."

Father Tom sat up. "What do you mean, payment?"

"I don't know how to say this, but...he wanted a cat."

Father Tom thought about the recent surge of signs posted around Riverview. His stomach churned as he thought of the grainy pictures, some offering rewards, some just begging for help. These were family pets, pets with names. They belonged to the boys and girls he preached to on Sundays. He groaned, prayed silently, and then asked, "You sacrificed cats?"

"No."

"Thank the Lord," Father Tom said, slumping in relief.

"I mean, not right away. See, these editors kept calling me, e-mailing me. Then eight checks arrived in three days. Checks for my stories. Stories I'd written. I couldn't let it stop, I had to do it."

Despite all his training, Father Tom found himself becoming emotional. "You sacrificed cats?"

"It's not like you think. I didn't carve them up on an altar and dance around naked under the full moon. At first, I'd just wait outside the dump and lure strays into potato sacks with catnip. Once I had one, I'd leave the sack in the cellar. Then, when the demon was done, I'd bury the corpse or wrap it in newspaper and send it out with the trash. It wasn't until later I drove around looking for cats people had put out for the night."

Father Tom found himself trembling, nauseated. This was not some freak on the five o'clock news he would work into a cautionary sermon, this was Adam, and Adam had cracked.

"You need help," Father Tom said. "There's this place I know. They're good at keeping things quiet."

"Tommy, you're helping me just by being here. I don't need anyone else." Adam glanced toward the cellar door. "Besides, it's hard for me to leave. He doesn't like it."

"Listen, let me take you there. I won't tell anybody you killed the cats. Nobody has to know."

"I told you, I didn't kill them, he did." Adam grunted and waved his hand in the air, as though shooing a bug. "They're not the point, anyway. Who cares about the damn cats? That's not why I called you."

Father Tom thumbed his temples. "Why, then?"

"Because it wasn't enough to just sell my short stories. You know what I wanted, what I've always wanted--to write books. Novels."

Father Tom remembered his best friend holding court over the neighborhood kids. Adam always told stories--at sleepovers, around campfires, at scout meetings, on the way to and from school. Everyone assumed he would grow up to be a writer. He had the amazing ability to incorporate his surroundings into his stories, sucking in the listener, getting him to ignore obvious explanations in favor of irrational, mystical, and supernatural ones. The hoot of an owl became a psychopath's signal to his accomplice. An exploding pine knot, a sniper's near miss. Rustling trees, an approaching army of giants.

The magnitude of Adam's gift became clear when Tom's little brother, Danny, came down with leukemia. Adam became a regular at the hospital. He visited Danny almost daily, sitting next to him in that sterile white hospital room, spinning an epic yarn.

In the tale, Danny wasn't dying, he was being pulled away to a world called Shim. The people of Shim needed him to lead a group of rebels against the evil, sorcerer overlord.

The story went on for months, and toward the end, the nurses and sometimes the doctors found excuses to come in and listen. As Danny wasted away on Earth, he grew in power on Shim, and the day before he passed away, he defeated the overlord and ascended the throne of Shim.

Tom couldn't cope with becoming an only child at age fourteen, so Adam resumed his tales of Danny's adventures. But that didn't stop the depression, the skipping of school, the fistfights, or the secret drinking. Nor did it prevent Tom from swallowing a whole bottle of sleeping pills.

But as he lay in bed waiting for sleep to take him forever, Tom kept thinking about how Danny was trying to root out a traitor among his advisors, each of whom had saved his life repeatedly during the ongoing defense against the invaders from the faraway continent of Maeror. If Tom were gone, Adam would stop telling stories of Shim, and Danny would be dead for good. In both worlds.

Tom couldn't let that happen. He had run to the bathroom and stuck his finger down his throat to spew out his insides, heaving himself dry.

After that, life slowly improved. He stopped stealing booze, his grades picked up, and Danny's army repulsed the forces of Maeror.

As they grew older, Adam written stories were continually rejected, and eventually he stopped talking of becoming a novelist. It had been years since Adam had even spun a yarn, but Father Tom realized that was exactly what he was doing now, and as always, Adam was folding real-life events into the tale. He wasn't an insane cat-murderer, he was a storyteller again.

Father Tom felt tension drain from his body. He wanted to laugh with joy, but he knew it would unravel Adam's yarn, so he stood and gathered the trash from the table once more.

Adam looked up, raised an eyebrow.

"I'm just cleaning up. I'm listening, though. Go on."

"Well, I figured since my stories were finally selling, perhaps my book might, too. It wasn't getting any better locked in the drawer, so I sent it off to Bantam, down in the city. It was pretty stupid. I mean, I had no agent, and I had sent it to their corporate headquarters, which I found out later is nowhere near the editorial department."

"You wrote an entire book in the last few weeks?" Father Tom asked, as he peeled open a large, black trash bag.

"Of course not," Adam said. "I sent them Floral Armageddon."

"The one where the aliens come down and bring the plants to life? Where the entire population of Hawaii is wiped out by angry pineapples?"

Adam's face reddened. "Yeah, that one."

"That book was awful. You said so yourself."

"Yeah, but look at all the garbage they publish nowadays."

If Father Tom had any lingering doubts about this being a yarn, they were gone now. Adam generally refused to acknowledge the existence of Floral Armageddon, and he would never send it to a publisher.

"Anyway, four days after I sent it, Sheldon Katz, Senior Editor at Bantam, called. He loved the book, said it was a sure hit and promised to get me a contract immediately.

"He wasn't kidding, either. The next day, a rep. from Bantam showed up. He had me sign a contract, and then handed me a cashier's check for one hundred and fifty thousand dollars. Three times what I make in a year, for something I wrote ten years ago.

"It was a dream. I could quit my job and write full-time. I pictured the book tours, the radio interviews, the modest way I would write personal notes to each fan at book signings. I might have stood there all afternoon, practicing my signature with an air pen," Adam said, waving his hand through the air, signing imaginary paper, "if he hadn't interrupted. He said only two words, but that was enough. Enough to shock me back to reality and destroy my life. Two little words."

At the sink, where he was scraping dishes and loading them into the dishwasher, Father Tom listened, but Adam said nothing. Adam had baited him, and it had worked. Father Tom needed to know those two words. He turned and asked, "What--"

"Your wife," Adam said, a tear spilling from his eye. He turned away and whispered, "Your wife."

Father Tom crossed the kitchen and reached out.

"Don't!" Adam snapped over his shoulder. "Just let me finish."

Adam took a deep breath and continued. "I knew what he wanted, but I wouldn't pay. The price was too high."

Father Tom heard anguish in Adam's voice. It was hard to stand by and do nothing, but he knew this was part of Adam's catharsis.

"Helen was at Emily DeMarco's that day, scrapbooking. I had no idea how far the demon's power reached, but I couldn't chance it, so I grabbed my keys and raced out to the car. The second I was outside, my head started throbbing. I floored it all the way down Main Street, right past Town Hall and your church. By then, the throb was a full-blown migraine. As I was about to turn on School Street, I had to pull over for an ambulance. When it turned down School, I just about died. I rode its tail so close, I passed the DeMarcos' and had to turn around.

"I turned wide, ended up on the lawn, and barreled through the front door screaming Helen's name. I was surrounded by all these women with their scissors and albums and coffee cups and stacks and stacks of pictures. They were all looking at Helen, and she was glaring at me. I grabbed her and dragged her out to the car, stammering something.

"Once we were in the car, she laid into me, but I heard nothing through the pain. I told her about the advance, and that we were going straight to the airport to take a trip to celebrate. Anywhere she wanted, even her mother's in Florida. Dear God, the pain was intense."

Adam grabbed his drink, downed it, shook his head, and sighed.

"She'd forgotten her wallet in her other purse. How anybody can leave the house without ID is beyond me, but we came home to get it, and I made her promise to stay in the car.

"The second I was inside, the headache vanished. I ran upstairs, and just as I grabbed her purse off the dresser, I heard the screen door slam. 'Let's go to Paris,' she shouted. 'I'll get the passports.' Our passports are in a shoebox in the cellar.

"I raced downstairs, yelling at her to get out, but I was too late.

"The cellar door was wide open, and she was still screaming when I reached the kitchen. It was pitch black down there. I flipped the switch, but no lights came on. As soon as I put my foot on the top stair, she made an awful gurgling noise, and the screaming cut out.

"I fell backward into the kitchen and just lay there, his stench and the sound of his breathing drifting up from below. I don't know how long I stayed there crying, sobbing, contemplating suicide."

Upon hearing the word "suicide," Father Tom spun, barking his shin on the open dishwasher. The pain raised his voice to a shout as he said, "You'll go to Hell!"

"That must have hurt," Adam said. "Come sit."

Father Tom hobbled over and rubbed his shin. He reminded himself this was only a yarn, part of Adam's coping process, although he was astounded that Adam had made Helen's death into a horror story.

"I won't lie to you, Tommy. I thought about killing myself, I really did. But I started thinking that's exactly what he wanted. I mean, he easily killed Helen, but for some reason, he hadn't touched me. I thought maybe he couldn't, and it gave me strength. I shouted at him, taunted him, dared him to kill me, but he didn't even respond.

"In the end, the phone snapped me out of it. It was the agent the Bantam folks had hooked me up with. They wanted to make Floral Armageddon into a movie . I told him to do whatever he wanted and hurried off the phone to call the police.

"I expected him to kill the Sheriff and the medical examiner, but he seemed to vanish while they examined and removed Helen's body.

"When they left, I decided to leave, too. Just take my advance and get out. But the second I was outside, the migraine came rushing back. It expanded like a balloon with every heartbeat, splitting my skull from the inside. I stumbled to the car, but was so crushed by pain I couldn't hold the key and finally had to retreat back inside.

"That's when I realized I was a prisoner, trapped in my own house. I can't even get the mail without my head feeling like it'll explode."

The bells at St. Catherine's began their top-of-the-hour cadence.

When the twelfth knell faded, Father Tom stood and said, "I have to conduct Mass at 12:30. Go clean yourself up, you're coming."

"I told you, he won't let me leave."

"Uh-huh, but you made it through the funeral just fine. Did he give you a pass on that, or did I maybe find a hole in your story?"

"Ken Spencer drove me to the funeral. I was totally doped up on Vicodin. Even so, by the time we left the cemetery, the pain was overwhelming the drugs, and I was ready to jam something through my ear."

"Okay, but while I'm poking holes, what about the check? If you went into the bank with a check that big, everyone in town would know."

Adam pulled a balled-up piece of paper from the pocket of his filthy dress pants and pushed it across the table. Father Tom flattened it out and saw it was a check made out to Adam for "one hundred fifty thousand dollars and zero cents."

"You said you submitted it to Bantam. This says Random House."

"They own Bantam," Adam said. "You don't believe me, do you?"

"The check's really nice. You can do amazing things with computers today," Father Tom said as he dropped the check on the table. "Don't get me wrong, I love the story, and I feel so blessed you chose to share it with me, but no, of course I don't believe you. Also, it feels unfinished. I mean, what, you're stuck in the house for the rest of your life? That's pretty weak."

"It's not finished."

"It's not? Well, I need to be there in less than half an hour, and you need to at least change your clothes, so tell me quickly, how does it end?"

Adam fished a hair off his tongue, wiped his fingers on his shirt, and said, "I couldn't live as a prisoner, yet I didn't think it was my time to die--God's plan and all that--so I asked him the price to be free."

Father Tom waited for Adam to continue. He waited for what seemed like forever before saying, "Come on, we don't have time for you to bait me. What was the price? What did he want?"

"A first-born virgin."

Father Tom laughed and clapped. "Of course! Why didn't I think of that? What else could it be? Now that is a good ending." He snorted. "You know, you are truly gifted. I came over to help you, but all I really did was listen while you helped yourself. It's just like with Danny, and, uh--with me, too." Father Tom put his hand on Adam's shoulder. "Your stories saved my life, Adam, and whether or not they make you rich, nothing will change that."

Adam lowered his head, said nothing.

Father Tom shook off the seriousness of the moment, and snickering, said, "Anyway, what're you going to do, lure a nubile young girl into your house and toss her into the cellar?"

Adam looked up, tears running down his face. "What? No, I--" He looked everywhere but at Father Tom. "I planned something else," he said, voice cracking.

Father Tom pulled Adam to his feet and hugged him closely, tightly. As Adam sobbed against him, Father Tom realized his friend was letting go of his fantasy, letting the truth about Helen sink in.

"It'll be alright. You'll get through this," Father Tom said. "We'll get through this."

Adam mumbled something.

"What?" asked Father Tom.

Adam lifted his head, sniffed, and ran his arm under his nose. "You've got to get out of here."

"I can stay a few minutes. We've still got time."

"No, you don't understand," Adam said, pulling away. "You've got to go." He shoved Father Tom toward the side door. "Go! Get out!"

An explosion shook the house like an earthquake. Bottles rolled off the table and smashed on the floor. The window over the sink shattered, raining glass on the counter. Bits of plaster tumbled from the ceiling, and Father Tom fell against the table as Adam dropped into his chair.

"I think your furnace just blew."

"Please, you need to get out. He's angry."

"What? The demon? Cut it out, Adam. The story's over." Father Tom hauled Adam out of the chair by his grimy shirt. "Come on. The whole cellar's probably on fire. Let's go."

Adam pulled away. "He won't let me leave, but it's not too late for you," he said, pushing Father Tom toward the side door again. "Get out while you still can. I'm sorry I lured you here, sorry for everything."

"There's no demon!" Father Tom shouted, shoving Adam aside and reaching for the cellar door. "Look, I'll show you."

"No!" Adam cried. He grabbed for Father Tom, but slipped and fell.

Father Tom whipped the door open, pulling an acrid, black cloud into the kitchen.

"See? There's noth--"

In the split-second before he was yanked into the cellar, Father Tom realized he had made a terrible mistake.

Adam lowered his head and closed his eyes. He heard a heavy thump. Then another. He wept when the screaming started.

When the screaming finally stopped, Adam was still crying. He cried for a long time before something from the depths of the cellar rasped, "Freeee."

Adam opened his eyes, stood up, and kicked the cellar door closed. He ran his hands along the length of his face, rubbing away tear-streaked dirt and grime. He looked around his filthy kitchen, and then walked in a daze up the short hallway past the parlor to the front door. He put his hand on the tarnished brass knob, and then let go, crossed himself, mumbled a quick prayer, opened the door, and stepped out onto the porch.

He stood motionless, eyes closed, waiting for the pain to tear through his skull. He counted slowly to fifty. To one hundred. The pain didn't come. He was free.

He inhaled deeply. Cherry blossoms, freshly turned earth, decaying grass. He heard children shouting and laughing, a lawnmower buzzing in the distance. He opened his eyes. The sky was a cloudless deep blue.

He took a step, and then another, testing the ground beneath him. He went to the end of his front walk. He planned to walk forever. Then he remembered something he had said to Tommy, and looking at the house--daring it to interfere--Adam opened his mailbox, spilling its contents onto the sidewalk. Among the bills and catalogs was a large, white envelope with a Madison Avenue return address.

Adam tore it open and pulled out a copy of the contract he had signed. Clipped to the top page, a handwritten note from Sheldon Katz read, "Loved it! What's next?"

Adam stared at the note for a full minute, and then walked up his front walk, entered his house, walked past the parlor to the kitchen, opened the cellar door, and called down to the demon, "How about a five-book series, instead?"

ABOUT THE AUTHOR

Dale T. Phillips has published novels, over 20 short stories and several story collections, poetry, and a non-fiction career book. He's appeared on stage, television, and in an independent feature film, Throg. He competed on Jeopardy and Think Twice. He's traveled to all 50 states, Mexico, Canada, and through Europe.

Connect Online:
Website: http://www.daletphillips.com
Blog: http://daletphillips@blogspot.com
Twitter: DalePhillips2

Other works by Dale T. Phillips

Zack Taylor Mystery Novels
A Memory of Grief
A Fall From Grace

Story Collections
Fables and Fantasies (Fantasy)
Crooked Paths (Mystery/Crime)
Halls of Horror (Horror)
Strange Tales (Weird, Paranormal)

Non-fiction Career Help
How to Improve Your Interviewing Skills

For more information about the author and his works, go to:
http://www.daletphillips.com

Made in the USA
Middletown, DE
30 December 2021